A

Truth

AND A

Lie

V. SOUSA

This one is for me: You fucking did it.

"Decode"—Paramore

"Ride Slow"—Russ

"Love You Twice"—Lilla Vargen

"Seven Devils"—Florence + The Machine

"Us"—James Bay

"Out of Love"—Alessia Cara

"Unfair"—6lack

"Forgiveness is not always easy. At times, it feels more painful than the wound we suffered, to forgive the one that inflicted it. And yet, there is no peace without forgiveness."
Marianne Williamson

A Truth
AND A
Lie

Prologue

I WAS ALWAYS TOLD THAT TO BE PART OF THE MAFIA, YOU needed a gun and a cold heart.

There is no room for love in this kind of life, and I know that.

It's like an unwritten code in the nonexistent handbook on how to successfully run a crime family.

"Love is a weakness," my grandfather would tell my brother and me. "It will be your biggest ruin."

I used to think he was crazy and had no idea what he was talking about, especially considering he worshiped his wife and absolutely loved his kids.

Growing up, men of power always surrounded me, and they all had a weak spot. I would see the meanest of men show mercy to the people who said just the right things, show affection to their wife or children, especially my father, who was head of the Romano crime family of Chicago.

Going back to 1921, my great grandfather, Dominic Romano, had moved himself and his whole family to America from Italy to start a bootlegging business with some of his brothers, and he was the best of the best.

He was more of a no-nonsense, shoot first, and ask questions later type, so his business was extremely successful.

If you ask me, though, I think he was just trigger happy.

Since the twenties, my family has just gotten into bigger and more illegal things, from guns to strip clubs. You name it, we deal it.

Some would call me fortunate to grow up in a family with so much money and power, but that's all they care to see.

I would've told you I had a perfect life at one point in time, but that was up until I found out a rival family brutally murdered my brother Samuel.

From then on, I hated everything to do with the mafia and, most days, my family too.

Sammy was my best friend, and he meant the world to me. We had been inseparable since birth. They say twins share a piece of their soul. He took a part of me with him that night he died, and I've never been the same since.

My brother died on October twenty-fifth—our birthday.

"Love is a weakness," my grandfather would always tell us.

I should've listened.

CHAPTER
One

Rose

Eighteen Years Old

I've ALWAYS DESPISED THE CONCEPT OF FUNERALS.

You get dressed up from head to toe in black clothes to watch as someone you know and love gets buried.

My family has had to attend countless funerals throughout the years, so maybe that's the reason I hate them so much.

I always felt sorry for the closest family members who stand in the front, not for their loss but for the fact that they have to force a smile and nod whenever they hear the repetitive "I'm sorry for your loss."

Death can bring you to your lowest point, and in the days that follow, you have to stand in front of a bunch of people, not once but twice, and try to hold back your emotions while your world crumbles in front of your eyes.

A two-part "celebration of their life" where you must entertain and thank every single person for attending.

I think the worst part, though, is that from then on, whenever you think of the person who has died, it will always come back to that damn funeral, and all you'll be able to see is their lifeless body lying in a casket.

It's a trick of the mind, really.

You pay people to make your loved ones look like they're peacefully asleep to try to ease the pain, but the harsh reality is that they're not sleeping at all, and you'll never see them again.

Everyone is entitled to their own opinion, and maybe my problem is that I get too invested in people. I should just skip a step and keep my distance from others. That way, it won't hurt so much when they leave you again, because they will. Everyone will, eventually.

Of the hundreds of people surrounding my brother's casket, I can only say that there are about half a dozen who truly knew him.

For the brief amount of time I give them my attention, they all looked back at me with pity and confusion written on their faces, and I fucking hate it.

They're probably wondering why I'm standing here looking up at the sky, not once looking down or at what's happening in front of me.

I refuse to look at the casket. I can't even tell you whether it's open or not, or even what it looks like. Either way, I will not let this be my last memory of him.

So, instead, I think of all the happy moments, remembering his smile and the last conversation I had with my other half.

I'd give anything to talk to him just one more time, tell him how much I love him, even just to hear his voice again. But that's the thing about death. You'd give everything to have one more conversation, but you know it would never be enough.

Life's a tough bitch, and she'll always win the fight. I learned that one the hard way.

CHAPTER
Two

Rose

"WHAT ARE YOU DOING, ROSIE BEE?" I HEARD MY brother ask from behind me. "You shouldn't be out here by yourself so late." I looked up at him from where I was lying in the grass and smiled.

"I'm looking at the moon and the stars, Sammy. They're so bright and beautiful tonight. Come lay with me if you're so worried about me being alone."

He lay down beside me and shifts his gaze to mine. "What's wrong, Bee? Why are you out here?"

"Are you sure you have to go to New York with Papa? You're going to miss our birthday, and I have a bad feeling about this."

"I'll be right back. Don't worry. It's only for three days. If you miss me"—he pointed at the star closest to the moon—"I want you to look at our star, or you could just call me. Either way, I'll be back for our birthday."

"Pinkie swear?" I held my pinky out to him.

"I promise, Bee." And he wrapped his pinky around mine.

My eyes flew open, and I frantically looked around the room.

I loved hearing my brother's voice. Sometimes the dreams felt so real, and for those few seconds, everything was okay again, but then reality set in, and I was still alone.

I wiped the tear that had fallen, then rubbed my wrist with my honeybee tattoo and read his writing—*I love you, Bee.*

Whoever said this got easier was full of shit.

"Rose," my mom called from outside my door, interrupting my thoughts.

I got up and ran to the mirror to make sure I got rid of any evidence of tears before she saw me. "Come in," I said as I quickly got back under the blankets.

My mother slowly opened my bedroom door and looked around my room. She was just now seeing all the changes I'd made in the past two years, which was how long it had been since she was last in here.

She tried to move a laundry basket filled with paints that I'd left in front of my door, but it was too heavy for her, so she just frowned and went around it.

She had gotten weaker in the last couple of years.

Her green eyes weren't as vibrant as they used to be, and her long black hair wasn't as shiny as it once was.

She'd always been short and relatively skinny, but she had lost so much weight that now her bones stuck out severely.

I found myself frowning, and in return, she forced a smile at me but didn't come any closer—probably fearing I would continue my inspection of how unhealthy and sad she looked.

I rarely saw her anymore, and when I did, it was like once or twice a month at the most, which was sad considering we lived in the same house.

"I've been knocking for five minutes. It's time to get up. Your father's guests will be here in a few hours, and you need to be up and ready," she said softly, practically in a whisper.

Perfect. Just how I wanted to spend my night—entertaining guests.

"Why do I have to be present for this again? I never have to be part of these dinners, so what's so special about this one?"

I guess that wasn't a good question because, in return, I got nothing but a sad smile. Then again, that was pretty much all I ever got out of her these days.

"I'll be down in time," I said as she walked out the door.

I grabbed my phone and looked at the time—10:48 a.m.

That meant I had seven hours until Papa's guests arrived, and I had to plaster my perfect daughter smile on my face and pretend that my life was peachy.

Six hours later, I was showered, dressed, and finishing up my hair when there was another knock on my door.

Two in one day? That was a record.

"Principessa, you in here?"

"Yes. Come in, Papa."

My father walked in, dressed to kill, and gave me a wide smile.

Whenever I watched the old mafia movies, the boss was almost always an old, short, bald guy who ate all the time and never got his hands dirty, but not my father.

In fact, John Romano was a very handsome man with his brown hair and dark brown eyes. He was well over six feet and more in shape than I could ever hope to be.

He and Sammy looked so similar that others actually

thought they were twins, which was saying something about my father's appearance considering their twenty-six-year age difference.

I felt him staring at me for a while before he finally spoke up. "Now, I'm sure I don't have to remind you that you need to be on your best behavior tonight," he said in his perfect Italian accent. "I have some important people I need you to be friendly with, and I can't have you acting out of character."

I didn't know if I should be offended or not.

It took a lot of hard work to sit there and pretend you were the happiest person in the world, that everything was perfect, and I thought I did a pretty damn good job.

"Don't worry, Papa. I'll behave," I said with a full smile, still not looking in his direction.

He sighed, and then I heard him walking back to the door. "Thank you, principessa. I love you. You look beautiful."

"Thanks," I said as he closed my bedroom door behind him.

It was sad to say that these days, I couldn't seem to look my father in the eyes.

On the harder days, I couldn't even bring myself to look at him at all. Not only because his appearance was so close to Sammy's that it almost physically hurt to look at him, but I just couldn't wrap my head around the fact that he was still happily continuing business despite what was done to his only son.

No money was worth losing a loved one. I liked nice things as much as the next person, but I would trade it all to get my brother back.

Turning off my curling iron, I slipped on my dress for the evening and gave myself a quick pep talk before leaving the safety of my bedroom.

I was on my way downstairs when I heard my mother and father in the kitchen whisper-yelling. I hadn't heard them talk to each other in a long time, so it took me a minute to get over my initial shock and process what they were saying.

"John, she's not ready. She's too young. Please don't do this," my mother begged.

"It's out of my hands, Maria. It's now or never."

I tiptoed the rest of the way down the steps. I was just about to walk in and ask them who they were talking about when someone grabbed me from behind.

I started to scream, but a hand was quickly put over my mouth, silencing me.

I managed to wiggle out of their grasp quickly, and was about to go into fight mode, but when I turned around to get a look at who was grabbing me, I nearly fell over.

Well, look at what the cat dragged in. None other than the enemy—Emmett Rossi.

Judging by appearance, the two years it'd been since I'd seen him last were very good to him.

Twenty-one-year-old Emmett was much more mouthwatering than the nineteen-year-old version.

He'd gotten taller—he must be at least six and a half feet now. His hair was still the same shade of dark brown, and hot damn, his muscles were huge. His arms were now littered with tattoos; one even went up his arm, under his shirt, and up his neck.

My lips started to involuntarily part but only for a minute before I slammed them back together. Ugh, I needed to relax before I started drooling. I hated how I was still very much attracted to him even after what he'd done to me.

I was blatantly looking him up and down, and when I finally reached his eyes, I held in a sad sigh at their color. Those eyes had always had a way of making me melt. I could always tell what kind of mood he was in just by looking into them. Naturally, they were a beautiful shade of amber, but his eye color was always changing.

My favorite was when they became more of a lighter blue; he was always able to tell me he loved me just by looking at me with those beautiful blues.

Looking at them right now, though, they were black. I used to hate when his eyes were black. They were always that color after he got back from visiting his father in New York. It was like he would put a wall up and devoid himself of all feeling, making his eyes turn as dark as he felt.

Two years ago, I was madly in love with him, and if you had asked me then, I would've told you he felt the same way. But looking back, he dropped me so quick it still makes me wonder if any of what I'd thought was even real.

All the promises he'd made and the declarations of love, I now questioned. He had been my world, and I'd thought we would be together for the rest of our lives, but that was a different time. I was blinded by love and by him. Weak.

Deeply and madly in love with him. But now? All I felt toward Emmett was disgust and betrayal.

It was crazy to think that Sammy and I had been best friends with him ever since we were young. Most would say that you wouldn't see one of us without the other two right behind.

Two hours after my brother was buried, Emmett had stared at me with black eyes and told me he was no longer in love with me, that he couldn't fake it, that it wasn't fair to him or me to stay in a loveless relationship.

I never saw him again after that. He became nothing but a memory, a ghost of the past—until now.

I tried to deliver a swift kick to his balls, but I wasn't nearly as trained as he was, so my attempt at saving his future wife from having to carry his spawn was quickly diverted.

"Get your filthy hands off me, or I'll scream," I said through clenched teeth when he grabbed my arms and pressed me against the wall.

"Go ahead. I'm sure your father would be thrilled about you eavesdropping on him."

I managed to break free of his hold again and gave him the meanest glare I could muster.

"You haven't been around for a long time, Emmett. Things have changed," I responded with a snarl.

"They're about to change a lot more," he countered.

I opened my mouth to ask him what he was talking about, but he turned and walked toward my father's office without another word.

After two fucking years, he just glided in and didn't even look the slightest bit affected about seeing me after all this time.

Meanwhile, I was over here, feeling like my heart was being ripped out all over again.

Love is a weakness. I repeated the mantra in my head.

Dinner was going to be a blast.

After I'd finally had a minute to think about what Emmett had said, I was more confused now than I was when he'd initially said it. Emmett had never been the type to be cryptic. Not only that, but what could he possibly know that I didn't?

Like clockwork, it hit six, and I was summoned with a knock at the bathroom door.

"Hurry. Everyone's waiting," my mother said through the door.

I opened the door and looked at my mother with a big smile planted on my face. "Let's go join the shit show!"

She didn't think that was funny—tough crowd.

Walking into the dining room, following behind my mother, I spotted Emmett sitting by my father, but I stopped short when I heard the voice of the devil himself, Emmett's father, Vincent Rossi.

Remember the old ugly mafia boss from the movies? That was him. Although he still had all his hair, give it a few years though, and I was sure he would have lost most of it.

Thank God Emmett got his looks from his mother, not that it mattered now anyway. He might be beautiful on the outside, but his inside was hideous.

"Nice of you to finally join us, Rose," Vincent said with a huff just as I stepped into the room.

He'd never liked me, and I was perfectly okay with that. I honestly think the majority of the reason Vincent disliked me so much was because I was almost the same height as he was— he at five foot five, and me at five foot four. It's a punch to the male ego when they feel short, especially to this sexist asshole.

"I wouldn't miss it for the world, Mr. Rossi," I replied with the fakest smile I could, and of course, that earned a nasty look from father.

Now, I know I said I was good at pretending I was friendly at these types of dinners, but Vincent was an exception.

It was bad enough I had to sit here and pretend like this man wasn't a major creep, whose eyes lingered a little too long when he looked at me, but my father was sadly mistaken if he thought I was going to be nice to any of the Rossi family members. Especially these two.

"Anyway," Vincent said, looking me up and down with a disgusting sneer, "now that Rose has finally graced us with her presence, I think it's time for the big news."

"Why don't we wait until after we eat?" my father suggested.

"Nonsense. There's no time like the present." Vincent smiled as he turned to Emmett.

He talked as if he was a king or something, all commanding and condescending. It took a lot of self-control not to point out the fact that if it weren't for his cousin being shot down, he wouldn't even be in the position of power.

I would have loved to knock him down a few pegs, but I didn't want to cause problems for my father.

Everyone stared at each other for what felt like forever, so, being impatient, I took my seat and turned to my parents. "Well, what is it?"

After another full minute of silence, my father cleared his throat. "Rose, I have arranged for you and Emmett to marry in six months as a sign of peace. The Romano's and Rossi's have shaken hands, and it's final."

It took me a few seconds to understand the bomb he'd just dropped on me.

I opened my mouth to say something but then shut it when I decided against telling everyone at dinner how I really felt about my father's "arrangement."

My father just gave me away to the enemy—to the family responsible for so many of the deaths of his closest friends.

He knew damn well I wanted no part of the mafia, and not only that, but he gave me to the boy who had ripped my heart out and left me there to bleed.

What kind of sick fucking game had my life turned into?

The worst part of it all was that no matter how much I fought it, I knew in the end, I'd have to go through with it.

I looked around and saw everyone staring at me, waiting for a response that they weren't going to get. Well, not tonight anyway.

The room began to spin, and I felt myself starting to sweat.

I had to get out of here. Fast.

I shot up from my chair with so much force that it fell back and hit the floor with a loud thud.

My mother flinched, and I watched as my father put his head in his hands. I looked at Emmett and saw that he was already looking at me with black eyes and no emotion in sight. Big shocker there. I shook my head and let out a huff of disbelief before I left the room.

I went right up to my bedroom, grabbed my keys, and walked straight out the door.

Fuck this.

CHAPTER
Three

Emmett

"WELL, THAT WENT AS WELL AS I EXPECTED," I said as a door slammed shut.

"She'll be fine. Probably just going for a run. She does that sometimes," John said, trying to sound nonchalant, but I could see the worry in his eyes.

"Well, we must be going. Try to keep your daughter under a tighter grip, John. Her attitude won't be a good accessory when she's married to my son," my father said in a tone that was meant to be serious but, in turn, just annoyed the fuck out of me.

"I'll walk you out," John said with a sad smile, getting up from his seat.

I was grateful that I had brought my car so I could follow Rose and make sure she wasn't doing anything reckless now that her father had told her, but I think I had a good idea of where she had gone.

I got a text from Rose's guard that confirmed my assumption.

Lorenzo: She just got to the cemetery.

Emmett: Thanks. On my way.

Pulling up to the cemetery, I saw her right away. She was lying at her brother's grave, looking up at the sky.

She came to the cemetery to visit her brother once a week, sometimes more, and every time she came, she looked up at the stars and talked to him for hours before she'd finally fall asleep.

From my usual spot behind a tree that was a few feet away from where she lay, I heard her speak.

"Remember when we were ten, and Emmett cut my ponytail? I ran to you, crying because it was almost time for my ballet recital, and I was so excited for Mom to curl my hair, but now, because of him, my hair was too short to curl, so you beat Emmett up so badly he didn't come to school for three days? Or the time that he put fleas in my sleeping bag when we went camping in the backyard, and you broke his nose?"

I let out a snort, hearing her rehash the dumb shit I used to do for her attention.

Sammy and I always fought back then when it came to Rose. He knew I liked her, but he always told me I wasn't ready yet and that I didn't deserve her, and he was right.

Rose used to be so sensitive when she was younger, and all those little pranks I'd pulled would make her cry for days, but I was a young boy who didn't know how to handle my crush and just wanted her to notice me.

The first time I saw her, I was transfixed by her beauty. Black hair, beautiful green eyes, a bright-ass smile, and dirt smeared all over her face.

She never noticed me when I first moved in. I had watched her and Sammy playing outside for a few days before I finally mustered up the courage to go to them.

Even at eight years old, I had told myself that I had to marry her and that I would do anything in my power to make that happen. But this wasn't what I'd meant when I said it.

My thoughts were cut off when she continued.

"Well, now I have to marry him, and you're not here to beat him up for me. I don't know what to do, Sammy. How am I supposed to marry into a world that I want nothing to with it? This life took you away from me. What if I fall for him again and the same thing happens? This isn't how my story is supposed to go."

I hated seeing her hurt like this, especially when I was the one who was the cause, but I had no choice in the matter either. It was either me or some other guy from my father's territory. Who knew what kind of person it would have ended up being?

I'd seen the cold, defiant look in her eyes earlier, and most mafia men thought beatings made women obey. I wouldn't be able to live with myself knowing she was getting beaten every day. I'd rather she be forced to marry me and hate me. At least that way, I knew she'd be safe.

I lowered myself to the ground, sitting against a tree, and listened as she talked and cried for another hour before she finally fell asleep to the empty sounds of the cemetery.

When two a.m. hit, I quietly walked up to her and gently lifted her in my arms, being careful not to wake her. I cradled her to my chest and allowed myself to breathe in her beautiful scent of vanilla and honey.

Walking to her car, I opened the door and gently placed her in the back seat.

Even with her face all blotchy and her eyes puffy, I swear she was still the most beautiful girl I'd ever seen. It was moments like these that made me want to beg for forgiveness, but I knew I couldn't.

Sammy had been my best friend. I'd promised him that if anything ever happened, I would protect her, and I went and broke her heart two days after he died.

The hardest thing I'd ever had to do was watch the last tiny bit of light she had left in her eyes fade and be replaced with complete darkness.

Lorenzo drove my car the two blocks it took to get to Rose's house, and I carefully drove her and her car back, parking in her spot. Lorenzo went ahead of me, opening the doors so I could glide in without moving her too much and waking her up.

I placed her gently on her bed, and just as I was tucking her in, I heard footsteps coming closer.

Pulling out my gun and turning quickly, I found her mother standing there with tears in her eyes. She didn't even flinch at the sight of a gun pointed at her, but I didn't know if that was a good thing or a bad thing.

I quickly put it away and placed Rose's phone and keys on her nightstand.

I'd been fortunate enough to not cross paths with Mrs. Romano very often whenever I'd had a meeting with John. Every time I saw her, she just looked so defeated. All I could see was the cold, distant look in her eyes, and it saddened me. She was nothing like the woman who used to walk into a room and have everyone smiling and laughing in the first five minutes of her arrival.

I turned to leave, making sure to keep my head down, but her voice stopped me in my tracks.

"Every time she leaves, I wonder if it will be the last time I'll see her." She walked past me to her daughter and sat on her bed, gently moving Rosie's hair from her face. "She's become so detached. Tonight was the first time I've seen any real emotion out of her in months. She even tried to crack a joke, but I know it was all from anger. One of my children died, and the other lost herself."

Finally getting the balls to look at her, the only thing I could conjure up was a weak ass "I'm sorry."

Instead of answering, she just continued to brush Rosie's hair back and quietly sang to her.

I could never repair what had been broken in the Romano's, but I sure as hell could try my hardest to keep everything together.

I left the Romano's house, and just as the clock read three a.m. I was exhausted, so I decided to go to my old house across the street. That way I didn't have to drive the twenty minutes it took to go home.

Walking into the house, I was surprised to see my father's office door open and the light on. I thought he would have been on his way back to New York by now since he hadn't stayed in Chicago overnight for years, ever since his cousin died and he became one of the underbosses of the Rossi crime family of New York.

I tried my best to walk by without being noticed, and I was almost in the clear when I heard my father call me. Stopping mid-step, I turned and walked into his office.

"Yes?"

"Did you find the little brat?"

It took every ounce of control I had in me not to snap at him, and after about fifteen seconds of breathing, I could finally answer him without snapping. "Yeah, I called her father to collect her."

"I hope she knows she can't pull this shit when she's married to you. I can't wait for all the attitude she has to be stripped away when you're finished with her. Get to bed. We have business to handle tomorrow," he answered with a sadistic smile.

My father had this sick idea in his head that I was just like him. I played along most of the time, but only because I didn't want him getting suspicious.

"Yes, sir," I said as I turned and made my way out of his office toward my bedroom.

I'd never understood my father's dislike for the Romanos. I'd heard a rumor that it all started when my father and John were young. Supposedly, they'd fallen in love with the same girl, and she chose John. Personally, I didn't feel like my father was capable of love at all, so I didn't know if that story was true or not.

I would have liked to say my father was a loving person at some point in my life, but thinking back, there was never a time that I could remember my father showing me any kind of love or compassion. I guess it expected when you were the product of an affair.

Well, I called it an affair, but my father called it an "I can do whatever and whoever I please." Though, in Mom's defense, she hadn't known about Dad's wife until after I was born.

For a while, I'd thought it was just me he disliked. Then I saw my father with his wife and other kids, and I found he was just as cold toward them. I was told he had another child, a girl, but I'd never met her. I doubted he was any nicer to her either, though.

I guess I should have been grateful that I got to live with my mother eight hundred miles away from him. He often came to visit, and I had to visit him sometimes, but it was just my mom and me for the most part.

Growing up, my mom always taught me to be forgiving and kind, but throughout my life, I'd learned that some people didn't deserve forgiveness, much less kindness, and my father was one of those people.

I was ten years old when I first saw my father hit my mother. I flew into the room, throwing punches at him, and he laughed the whole time. When I finally tired myself out and stopped, he hit me so hard that I saw spots until I hit the floor.

After that, he made sure to lock me in my room when he felt like using her as a punching bag. I would have to hear her cry all night until he either knocked her out or she had no energy left to cry.

Seven years later, my mother was driving to pick me up from school for fighting this punk kid who'd grabbed Rosie's arm when Mom's car was shot at and set on fire.

An hour after she was killed, the principal pulled me into his office. When I first went into the office, I was confused because I didn't see my mom anywhere, but then he told me my mother had been in an accident. I asked him which hospital she was at, but he frowned and shook his head. He told me he was sorry and that she didn't make it.

I asked how he knew, and he told me that my father had called the school and asked if the principal could relay the message. I flew out of the office and ran all the way home, needing to see for myself that she was actually gone. I wanted this to be one of those tests my father put me through to "toughen me up." I was hoping that when I got home, I would see Mom in the kitchen, smiling at me, but when I got inside, she wasn't there.

I was walking to her library when I heard my father's voice coming from his office. I didn't even know he was visiting, so I quietly got closer to the door to make sure it was him and not some random person. When I stopped to listen, I heard him thanking someone, saying how glad he was that "she's finally out of the way" and that "all the money was there."

I didn't want to believe that my father would kill my mother. I knew he was a monster, but there was no way he would go this far, right?

I got my answer a few hours later when I realized he was gone. He'd come to Chicago and left without seeing me or even saying anything to me. If it weren't for me coming home early and hearing him in his office, I wouldn't have known he was even in New York.

He didn't even have the decency to show up to the funeral.

To this day, he has never mentioned my mother or her murder to me. It was as if she'd never existed. I knew they hadn't loved each other and were never really together, but I didn't think he hated her so much to the point of murder.

I don't know why he'd had my mother killed, and I didn't think I would ever find out, either.

I did know one thing, though. The first opportunity I got to kill him, I wouldn't think twice. Consequences be damned.

CHAPTER
Four

Rose

Sixteen Years Old

WE'D BEEN DRIVING FOREVER IN COMPLETE SILENCE. I hated when Emmett came back from his dad's. He got all quiet and moody, and it took him a solid week to get back to his usual self.

We were doing so good before he left that I had even thought he was going to ask me out, but now, seeing how he was acting, I didn't foresee that happening anymore.

I hated his dad. He ruined everything.

We pulled up to some woods, and he put the car in park before turning it off.

I turned to him and gave him a confused look, and he just blankly looked back at me.

He hopped out of the car and started walking, but when

He barely had my door open before I yanked it back and locked it.

I cracked the window open a tiny bit and frowned up at him. "Sammy knows I'm with you, so if you're here to kill me, I'm just warning you that your friendship is going to be over, and he will probably murder your ass."

I got a little laugh out of him before he shoved the key in my door and unlocked it, then yanked it open. "Don't be so dramatic, Rose. I want to show you something."

I contemplated not going, but my curiosity got the best of me, so I quickly got out, not giving myself time to change my mind.

"You know this is how they come up with horror stories," I rushed out, ducking when I heard leaves rustling over my head. "You're never supposed to go into the woods in the middle of nowhere at night."

He didn't respond, just pulled me behind him toward a trail entrance, and after walking uphill for ten minutes, we reached this huge clearing.

I was about to continue my shit talking but I was stunned into silence when I looked up.

The intense vibrancy of the moonlight lit the clearing, and the stars looked so close that I was tempted to reach a hand out and see what happened.

I could feel Emmett staring at me, probably waiting for me to say something, but this view had me at a loss for words.

"It's so beautiful. How did you find this place?" I asked, not looking away.

"Well, I know you like to look at the stars, so I got bored one day and went exploring." He pulled a blanket out of nowhere and laid it on the ground. He motioned for me to lay down, so

I awkwardly slid down onto the blanket, cursing my decision to wear such a short dress.

I didn't think this place could get any more perfect, but when I laid back and looked up, it did. This place just became my favorite place in the entire world, so I officially made this our spot.

"Oh, my God, Emmett, this is so beautiful." I finally looked away to turn to him and frowned when I noticed his eyes were black.

I looked away from him and let out a sad sigh. I wished he would just talk to me and tell me what was wrong.

"How was your dad's?" I asked.

"Fine."

I hated that I had to force it out of him, but he would be like this for a while if he didn't let it out now. "Emmett, what's wrong?"

He closed his eyes and let out a long breath. "Sometimes, I just wish my father would leave me be. He wants me to be just like him and go into business with him, but the last thing I want is to be tied to my father. There are so many things my father does that are unnecessary and just cruel. I don't know. I just wish he was more like your dad. I've always respected that your father keeps business away from you guys as much as possible and doesn't force it on you."

It broke my heart to see him so sad like this, but a part of me loved the fact that I was the only person who saw this side of him.

"I know what you mean. No offense, but your dad's an ass-hole," I said with a shrug.

He gave me a small laugh in response.

"See, there's that laugh I love to hear. If it makes you feel any better, my father has guards follow me around, and he thinks I don't know. I swear, the other day, one of them accidentally followed me into the bathroom."

"I wish it were that simple for me," he whispered.

I didn't know how to respond, so I just kept quiet.

It was silent for a little while, and it was starting to make me antsy. The silence made it so that you were in your own head, and that was when your thoughts took over, so I blurted out the first thing I could think of.

"Emmett, tell me a lie?"

I practically heard him roll his eyes. "Not this again, Rosie. You know I don't like this game."

"First of all, it's not a game. It's a form of communication, and second, it will grow on you, so hush up and tell me."

"Fine, but only one. I liked the shirt you wore to school today."

Well, that was rude. "Geez, if this is the lie, then I'm scared to hear the truth."

"You should be scared. I sure as hell am."

I waited for him to continue, but he never did, so I got pushy. "Well, go on, tell me your truth." I flicked his hand.

"I love you, Rose."

"Okay, I love you too, but tell me."

"No, Rose, I love you. That's my truth."

Was I missing something? "Huh?"

"I mean, I want to be with you. Boyfriend and girlfriend, and maybe I'm talking crazy, but I kind of want to marry you too. Not now because we're still young, but in the future. I talked to Sammy, and he's cool with it. He actually said, 'It's about damn time,' and he also threatened my life, but that's beside the point, and I'm rambling, but it's only because—"

I decided to put him out of his misery and put my hand over

his mouth. "Of course I'll be your girlfriend. It's about damn time," I said with the biggest smile.

He pulled me onto his lap and grabbed both sides of my face. "You're so damn beautiful." He ran his thumb along my bottom lip, and I melted into his touch. He slowly pulled me closer, and I leaned into him until, finally, his lips met mine. It took him a torturous full second before he deepened the kiss, and I let out a soft moan.

And I swear, in that very moment, everything felt right.

It was as if nothing could really be that bad because at least we had each other. Like, no matter what happened in life, it would always be okay—even if it was only for a little while.

CHAPTER
Five

Rose

I HAD ABOUT THIRTY SECONDS OF PEACE WHEN I WOKE UP this morning, but then everything that happened last night at dinner came rushing back to me and made me wish I was still asleep.

I honestly didn't know how to feel about this whole situation. I knew running out of dinner hadn't been the best way to go about it, but I didn't see that shit coming, and I'd just needed space before I said or did something crazy.

I had always figured I would be married off for tactical reasons, but after I turned eighteen, there was no more talk of marriage, so I figured it wasn't going to happen.

I used to hear whispers from the other bosses' wives, saying that the people my brother and I were being married off to had already been chosen for years.

After Sammy died though, the only whispers I heard were that nobody would want to marry such a broken girl. They all laughed when one woman mentioned that the men enjoyed breaking their wives in themselves, and me being in the state that I was in, took the fun out of it for them. Safe to say, I never when to another event after that.

I was really dreading leaving my bedroom and facing my parents, but delaying the inevitable was pointless, and it was time to put on my big-girl panties.

Of course, the minute I went down the stairs, I saw my father sitting in his office. He looked up at the sound of my footsteps and barked at me, "Rose, come in here, please."

I took my sweet-ass time walking in because I was pissed at him, which earned me a dirty look in response. Oh well.

"I will not have you embarrassing me like that again. It makes me look weak that my daughter does whatever she feels as if she has no consequences."

Now, I knew I was very fortunate because my father had never been the type to raise a hand to me, Sammy, or my mom, and he tried his hardest to give us the most normal life possible. The last thing I wanted was for him to look weak, but what did he expect me to do? Thank him?

"I'm sorry, but I wasn't expecting that," I said with a shrug.

"And I know that, but my hands are tied. The last thing I wanted for you was this, but I can't afford another war. Be grateful you get to marry Emmett and not someone you don't know."

He wasn't even giving me the option to say no to the marriage, practically telling me that if I didn't marry Emmett, there would be a war, and the lives lost would be on me. He knew exactly how to get me to go along with this. I would never be able to live with myself if people died because of a decision I'd made.

I was about to tell him that it wasn't fair to put that on me when he continued, "I thought you'd be happy considering you guys were such good friends growing up."

Little did my father know, Emmett and I were much more than "good friends."

Nobody other than Sammy and my best friend, Claire, knew that little piece of information, though.

"Things change. We haven't been friends for a while now."

"Very well, then. Like I said before, be grateful it's someone you know and not a stranger." This time, his voice was stern, telling me I needed to stop arguing.

I hadn't talked to Emmett since Sammy's funeral, so I think, at this point, it was safe to say that I really didn't know him anymore, so he might as well be a stranger to me. But I knew when I was fighting a battle I couldn't win, which this was, so there was no sense in me continuing it.

"You're right. I'm sorry I embarrassed you," I said through gritted teeth.

He nodded and straightened his shirt. "Just don't let it happen again."

Not knowing what else to say, I turned and walked out of his office and back to my room.

I needed to get out of this house. Everything that was going on was making me crazy.

Grabbing my phone, I texted Claire.

Rose: Hey, girl, any plans for tonight?

Claire and I had been friends since we were freshmen in high school.

One day, I was on my way to the cafeteria when I saw Emmett talking to Victoria Diego. She was captain of the cheerleading squad, blonde hair and blue eyes—the typical bitch that no one and everyone liked. Emmett had hooked up with her off and on for a while but broke it off a few months before.

Now, at this point, I would've liked to say that Emmett and

I were on our way to becoming more than friends, so seeing him with Barbie 2.0 was really a punch in the balls.

Not wanting him to see me hurt, I went into the bathroom, and, of course, Victoria followed me. She came up behind me while I was wiping my eyes and looked at me through the reflection of the mirror.

"He will never want someone like you. You're so boring and act like his little puppy dog." I wanted to laugh when she said that, like how much more cliché could this get.

Next, she was probably going to give me the whole "He's mine, so stay away from him" speech.

I turned around and was ready to give her my full wrath when out of nowhere, a girl with bright red hair flew out of one of the bathroom stalls and just punched Victoria dead in her face, causing her to fall on the nasty bathroom floor.

The girl turned to me and said, "I really can't stand the bitch." She let out a breath and stuck her hand out toward me. "My name's Claire," she said with a wink, and we'd been best friends since.

My phone started ringing, and I answered when I saw that it was Claire. I didn't even have time to say hello before she was talking.

"Now, I do. We're going to the club."

Ugh, I hated the club. Huge crowds of people made me paranoid, especially when under the influence of copious amounts of alcohol, but I guess it was either that or staying home all night, wallowing in my self-pity.

I'll take the club for two, please *(insert smiley face here)*.

"Okay, meet at my place?"

"I'll be there in an hour," she replied before hanging up.

An hour later, I spotted Claire walking up my driveway with a suitcase rolling behind her.

Here we go.

Opening the front door, I pulled her in before my father could see her in the security footage. "I thought we were going to a club, not on vacation?" I said in a rush.

"We need options. We're going to that new club that just opened downtown, which is twenty-one plus, so we have to look the part," she said with a wink. "I convinced Tommy to give us a ride, but I didn't tell him we were going to the club because we don't need him hovering."

Tommy is Claire's hot older brother, who had been friends with Emmett for years. Sammy too when he was alive.

Tommy's a little taller than six-foot, with dark brown hair, ocean blue eyes, and a killer fucking body. He looked like a pretty boy, but he had gotten into a few fights in my presence, and let me just say, he was extremely underestimated in all of them.

There had been a few times where I'd had to snap out of the trance that his mouthwatering figure had put me in, especially now that he was covered in tattoos.

"I haven't seen Tommy in forever. Why can't he hang out with us?"

"Because, Rose, he's friends with the enemy, and we don't associate with the likes of them," she stated.

Emmett and Tommy still talked to each other a lot from what Claire told me, but I couldn't hold it against Tommy because even though Emmett did me dirty, it didn't mean that he deserved a lonely, miserable life.

"Don't you think you're being a little overdramatic? He's

your brother. Besides, if I don't have a problem with him, you shouldn't have a problem either. Tommy's cool."

"I wasn't going to tell you this, but since you're being pushy"—she put her hands on her hips and huffed—"ever since Tommy has gotten back from summer break, he and Emmett have been hanging out almost every day, and I don't want to invite Tommy, and then Tommy invite Emmett."

Fair point. Moving on.

I really wanted to tell Claire about what was going on, but I knew she would ask a million questions, and tonight, I just wanted to drink and pretend like I wasn't being coerced into marrying Emmett Rossi.

Looking through the clothes Claire brought, I decided on a beautiful backless wine-colored sparkly dress that showed the perfect amount of boob.

I might as well go wild, considering in five months and twenty-nine days, I was going to be getting married.

I went into the bathroom to put the dress on when I heard Claire whisper-yelling on the phone. "What do you mean you're going to pick up Emmett? I told you to be here to pick us up at nine, and it's already ten." She must have been talking to Tommy.

I would have loved to have heard Tommy's response. He wasn't always the brightest bulb when it came to certain things.

"No, Emmett cannot go with you to drop us off. What is wrong with you? Just turn around and come get us—alone."

She must've hung up because the next thing I knew, she was barging into the bathroom. "Damn, girl, you clean up nice. If I were into girls, my face would be motorboating the shit out of your tits."

Looking at her outfit, she'd picked a cute plain wine-colored crop top and a jean skirt, an odd pair up, but like anything else, she pulled it off nicely.

"You're not looking so bad yourself. We kind of match."

She pulled two whiskey nips out of her bra and passed them to me. We silently cheered and threw it back, grimacing at the warm, spicy taste of cinnamon.

"Are you ready? Tommy's five minutes away," Claire said before moving to the mirror and doing a final check of her appearance.

"Yeah, let's head down now and meet him at the bottom of the driveway. I don't want my dad to see us."

Usually, I wouldn't care if my father saw me going out, but I didn't want him to tell Emmett I was going out all dressed up and make him suspicious.

By the time we reached the bottom of the drive, Tommy's Maserati was pulling up to the sidewalk, and he was rolling the window down.

"I thought I was bringing you guys to the movies. Why are you two dressed like you're about to go to a brothel?" he yelled at us from inside the car.

I didn't know if I should be insulted or if I should laugh. I knew my dress was a little skimpy, but I didn't think it was brothel skimpy.

I rolled my eyes at him and laughed. "Hello to you too, Tommy. Yes, it has been a while, and it's great to see you too."

"Oh, come on, Rosie, you know I still love you." He got out of the car and rounded the front, pulling me in for a big hug. "Just give me the word, and we can run away together." He lifted me, spinning us around a few times before gently placing me back on the ground and kissing me on the cheek.

"I'm ready right now if you want to go." I was only half-joking, of course.

Although running away with Tommy sounded much more

appealing than having to look at Emmett's stupid face every day after we were married.

Who was I kidding, though? If I were ever to run away, it would either be Emmett or my father hunting me down. They were very resourceful men, and the mafia made it so that they had fingers in every pie, my father more than Emmett, but I was sure the both of them would make it a team effort.

Claire shoved her arms between the two of us and used all her strength to push Tommy away from me. "First of all, ew, no, she will not run away with you. Second, just because we're going to the movies does not mean we can't dress up."

"Didn't that club just open up across the street from the theater?" He gave us a look that said he wasn't stupid.

Shit. We were busted.

"It's twenty-one plus, genius, and last time I checked, Rose and I still have a few months until then."

I'd always admired how Claire could talk us out of any situation. She had a way of mixing some truth with the lie and adding a dash of annoyance in her voice to make the other person feel stupid for even asking. I had no doubt in my mind that she was going to be able to get us into this club.

Tommy let out a huff of annoyance. "Fine. Let's go."

We all jumped in the car, and ten minutes later, we were pulling up to the movie theaters.

I took a quick look across the street to see the line outside of the club, and I was getting impatient just looking at it. I mean, it was a Sunday night.

Granted, it was a holiday weekend, but still, it was Sunday. Didn't anybody go to church anymore?

I could only imagine what this place looked like on a Friday or a Saturday.

"Thanks, bro," Claire said, slapping him on the shoulder. "I'll text you later to pick us up when the movie's done."

"Hold up. You never told me you needed a ride back too."

"Well, how else are we supposed to get back? Uber? Walk? Do you want us to get kidnapped?"

"Fine." He sighed in defeat. "I'll pick you guys up, but I have some things to take care of, so watch two movies or something."

"k bye" She slammed the door, and Tommy sped off.

Turning to me, she asked, "Are you ready?"

That was a loaded question if I'd ever heard one. "As I'll ever be, but first, we have to look and see where Lorenzo is. I don't want him telling my father that we're not at the movies but at a twenty-one-plus club instead."

Looking around both sides of the sidewalk, I spotted him leaning against a tree, and I marched straight up to him. It was better to come off abrasive. That way, he would think twice about arguing with me.

I popped out in front of him, and he quickly jumped back. I always enjoyed the look of shock he got on his face when I spotted him, and he thought he was incognito. Don't get me wrong, he was very stealthy and could keep quite a low profile, but I'd been dodging guards my whole life, so finding him was easy.

"Lorenzo," I said when he started to open his mouth.

"Rose." He cocked an eyebrow at me.

Lorenzo Moretti, my bodyguard for about six years now, tall as fuck, smooth tanned skin, black hair, and deep blue eyes that always looked like his thoughts were very far away from here, and most importantly, he was my other best friend.

"So, Claire and I are going to the club across the street, but if my father asks, I want you to confirm that we are at the movie theaters." I smiled at him.

Lorenzo pinched the bridge of his nose and huffed. "Not happening, Rose. You know I can't do that. Are you crazy?"

"See, I thought you would say that, so I'm prepared to offer you a deal. In return for your discretion, I won't tell Father about the 'break' you took the other day at the mall when you went to go fuck that blonde chick with the big boobs in the dressing room of Express. And before you say anything, yes, I knew, and no, I won't tell, but only if you don't tell him about this."

Lorenzo searched my eyes to see if I was bluffing or not. "Fine. But if he finds out, you have to say you threatened my life or something, and I'm going in with you, no disappearing on me when you get inside either."

"Deal." I held out my hand, but he was hesitant to shake it.

"Just shake it, for goodness sakes," I said, shoving my hand in his.

Reluctantly, he shook my hand and laughed. "Are you sure you don't want to take over when your dad retires? You'd be a really good asset."

Yeah, that was going to be a hard no from me. I gave Lorenzo a sharp "Positive" and grabbed Claire's hand.

He probably regretted his words because he gave me a sad smile and apologized.

I looked at Claire, still holding her hand. "You ready?"

"Yeah, let's go," she said, wearing the same sad smile as Lorenzo.

We checked to see if any cars were coming and made our way across the street. As I walked toward the end of the line, Claire grabbed my arm, tugging me in the opposite direction, toward the bouncer. "I am not waiting in that long-ass line. Follow my lead."

She walked right up to the bouncer and lightly grabbed his arm with a sultry smile. "Hey, handsome. So, my friend here and I were hoping you could let us skip the line. She and her boyfriend just broke up, and we're trying to have little fun, but I don't want to kill my buzz by sitting in the line." She said with a pouty face at the end to add to her little show.

The bouncer looked her up and down, then shifted his gaze to me and proceeded to look me up and down.

After his viewing or whatever you call it, he finally smiled and licked his lips. "Sure, baby, you got your ID's on you?"

Moment of truth…

"I do, but my birthday isn't for a few months, and as I said, I want to have a good time," she said with a wink.

He looked inside the entry of the club and then around us, "Fine, you can go in, but don't get yourselves into any trouble."

She gave him a big smile in return and kissed him on the cheek. "Thank you. I appreciate it, babe." She grabbed my hand once more and pulled me into the club.

I looked back to check on Lorenzo, and that's when I noticed that Lorenzo gave the bouncer a head nod and walked right in behind us with no problem.

I turned back to Claire to see if she'd noticed, but she was too busy looking around to have seen the exchange. "Hey, didn't you say this place just opened?" I yelled to her over the music.

It took a minute for Claire to understand what I was asking since it was so loud in here. "Yeah, why?"

That was weird. How would Lorenzo already know the bouncer? He definitely didn't work for my father because I'd never met him, and my father only ever dealt with clubs of the stripper variety.

We walked further into the club, and just as I had suspected, it was packed with people, bodies surrounded by bodies, sweating and breathing all over each other. On the plus side, though, this place was heavily air-conditioned and wasn't as hot as I'd expected. It was still hot as fuck, don't get me wrong, but not get me the hell out of here hot.

Claire pulled me straight toward the bar and ordered four lemon drop shots. She barely had the order out when I heard a guy to the left of us ask the bartender to make us two more shots on him.

And that brought us to reason number one of why I hated going to clubs. Guy buys girl a drink, and then girl feels obligated to dance with the said guy and/or talk to him as a form of thanks.

We downed all six shots easily because lemon drop shots went down like juice, but just as I thought we were in the clear with the guy and he wasn't going to talk to us, I heard him clear his throat loudly.

"You ladies come here often?" He must have gotten really close because I felt his breath gliding across the back of my neck as he spoke.

I turned around to look at him and was surprised to find that he was kind of cute—light brown eyes, dirty blonde hair pulled up into a man bun, and a smirk on his face.

I wasn't usually the type to flirt, but since everything was going to shit, I might as well throw all caution to the wind.

I gave him the sweetest smile I could conjure and shook my head. "No. This is my first time here. Thank you for the drinks, by the way."

"No problem," he replied. "You girls want another round?"

Claire wasted no time popping her head out from behind me and giving him a strong yes.

I guess he really wanted us drunk because he ordered another two shots for us and four shots of jack honey for himself and his friend that I just noticed was seated next to him.

He lifted his shot in the air and winked at me. "Cheers to new friends."

"Cheers," Claire said, and all four of us clinked our glasses together.

"I didn't catch you two beauties' names," the one next to me asked while putting his hand on the back of my chair.

"Well, I'm Rose, and this is Claire. And yours?"

"Landon and this is my buddy, Dave. You ladies wanna dance?"

Now, normally, I would politely decline, but I did just take four shots, plus the shots from earlier, so my ability to think clearly had gone out the window. I was definitely feeling them now. I looked at Claire to see what she thought, and when she got up and grabbed Dave's hand, I followed her lead and grabbed Landon's.

I looked back at the bar to make sure I didn't leave anything behind when I noticed the bartender staring at me and talking, but nobody was there, and he wasn't on the phone.

I was too drunk to put too much thought into it, so I turned back around and let Landon lead me away.

We were barely on the dance floor when Landon grabbed my hips and started aggressively grinding into me. I was instantly annoyed because he already had a hard-on, and I'd barely touched him. I didn't know what kind of girl he thought I was, but this definitely wasn't it.

I tried to pry his hands that were currently digging into my hips really hard off me, but he just dug them deeper.

He turned me around, grinding into the front of me, and slid one of his hands down to grab my ass, and I looked up to tell him to stop, but just as I was about to make eye contact, my eyes caught something else instead and I froze at the sight of Emmett charging right at me, looking murderous.

40

Oh, fuck.

There had only been a small handful of times where I'd seen Emmett mad, and let me tell you, it was a scary sight to see. Emmett was so good at keeping his anger at bay that when he finally did let it lose, it was best you kept your distance.

I jerked my head up to tell Landon to run, but I think he thought I was going in for a kiss because the next thing I knew, he was slamming his lips onto mine and biting my bottom lip so hard that I instantly tasted blood.

I pushed at his chest, trying to get him off me, but he just held on to me tighter. I brought my knee back, ready to go for the balls, when he was suddenly off me and on the ground in front of me.

Emmett was standing over Landon, breathing heavily with his fists clenched on either side of him, staring at him like a psychopath, not saying a word.

Landon opened his mouth, closed it, then opened it again. "Look, man, I don't want any problems. She came onto me, begging me to dance. I just agreed so she would stop asking," he stuttered.

What a pussy. He would never last in my world, and to think I thought he was cute.

Emmett jerked his head toward me with a hard glare. "Is that true?"

I laughed at the question. I wasn't even going to respond to that.

Maybe I was trying to avoid a fight between them, or honestly? Maybe I just wanted him to feel an ounce of the hurt that I felt. It even could be the fact that I was wasted right now, but when I looked up at him, all I saw were those black eyes, looking back at me with disappointment, so I shook my head and walked away.

I stomped outside like I was on a mission but then stopped when I realized I had nowhere to go. So instead, I just leaned against the building and waited for Lorenzo to come out so I could ask him to take me home.

I spotted the bouncer giving me the side-eye, and it all clicked as to how Emmett knew I was here.

I crossed my arms and glared at him. "You knew the whole time who I was." It was supposed to be a question but came out as a statement.

All the bouncer did was shrug his shoulders, so I continued, "So if I try to run away, are you going to tell him which direction I run in?"

He looked at me and nodded. *Well, at least he was honest.*

Giving up my fight, I sank down and sat on the sidewalk, not even caring that this was gross.

Lorenzo came out to find me a minute later, and once he saw me, he gave me an apologetic look and sat down next to me.

He opened his mouth, probably to apologize, but I didn't want to hear it, so I cut him off before he could say it. "Yeah, I know. I feel sorry for me too."

At least that lightened the mood a little and got a chuckle out of the both of us.

I was sitting with Lorenzo for what felt like forever when I heard Claire shouting from inside the club, and it was getting louder.

"So, what? You think you can just drag us out of here like we're children? You already broke her heart, so why not take her happiness too? Or is that your next task? Why don't you just put a leash on her so you can pull her back whenever she's being disobedient."

And that was why she was my one and only friend. She

would fight to the death for the people she cared about. You didn't get many of those these days.

Lorenzo quickly got up at the sound of Claire's voice and reached a hand out to help me off the ground.

She walked over to us just as I was getting on my feet. Emmett looked between the two of us with a glare, pointing to the street. "Get in the car. Now," he growled at us before going back into the club.

I followed where his finger was pointing and saw his car there. I was surprised I didn't notice it before since it wasn't an ordinary car you saw everywhere.

He'd had the same car since I was fifteen—a matte black 1970 Dodge Charger RT.

I remembered when he first got it. He was so excited when he showed Sammy and me, and all I kept thinking was, *Damn, this car looks like a hunk of shit*, but I never told him that. He'd rebuilt the whole engine with the help of Sammy and Tommy, and they'd cleaned up all the rust and repainted the whole car, making it look brand new.

During the summer, Emmett, Sammy, Claire, Tommy, and I would ride around for hours, going wherever the car would take us, just cruising.

I think that was the happiest I'd ever been in my life. I had everyone I cared about so close to me, and everything was so fun and carefree. It saddened me to think of all the shit that had changed and how I'd never again feel that happiness.

I didn't realize I was crying until I felt a tear hit my boob.

I could feel everyone's eyes on me, but my feet were frozen in place, and I just couldn't stop looking at that fucking car.

Someone lightly grabbed my arm, and then Claire stepped in front of me, blocking my view of the car.

"Come on, Rose. We should get out of here. I'm really tired."

I frowned and nodded my head at her. She sounded so sad, or maybe it was me, I didn't know. This was why I didn't drink.

She tugged at my arm, and I finally snapped out of it and moved toward the car.

I hated feeling all this emotion, but with Emmett showing back up in my life, it opened old wounds, and I couldn't get the bleeding to stop. I wiped my eyes one last time, and I hopped in the passenger seat with my head down.

Emmett stomped out of the club a few minutes later and flew into the driver's seat, slamming the door.

As we pulled away from the curb, I leaned my head against the window and closed my eyes.

I expected the ride home to be quiet, but I was obviously wrong because Emmett suddenly went off.

"Did you think that was funny? Going out dressed like a fucking prostitute and having some random guy practically fuck you on the dance floor. Was that fun?" He slammed his hand against the steering wheel when I didn't respond and continued, "Well, I hope it was good while it lasted because if you think I'm going to allow my fiancée to go around embarrassing not only herself but me as well in my own fucking club, then you're sadly mistaken because this is the last time you will be doing this. I fucking tried to be patient with you when you walked out on dinner, and I tried to give you the benefit of the doubt because this was sprung on you, but now you're just being fucking disrespectful."

Wow. What fucking nerve.

He popped back into my life twenty-four hours ago, and he thought he had some sort of claim on me?

Well, I hoped he had at least got off on his little rant because it was my turn now.

Letting out a crazed laugh, I turned to him and spewed the

venom at him that I'd been holding in for years. "You're joking, right? Who the fuck do you think you are? You aren't my
boyfriend, you sure as fuck are not my fiancé, and to be honest? You're not even my friend. You think you can order me
around? That's cute. Did you forget that *you* broke up with me?
I'm glad you're upset. You deserve so much worse than feeling
embarrassed."

I took a breath and gave him one last humorless laugh.

"I will never forgive you. I gave you everything I had in me,
and do you remember what you did?" I was met with complete
silence, so I continued, "Oh, you were so brave before, but where's
that now? It's okay. I'll refresh your memory. I gave you my vir-
ginity, and then not even twenty-four hours later, you broke up
with me at my brother's funeral. I lost the two most important
people in my life in a matter of three days.

"Maybe I'm just being a bitter bitch, but you have no right
to give me any shit for my decisions. Did you see what I was trying to do back at the club? I was trying to pry his hands off me
because his fingers were digging into me so hard that there are
probably bruises now. So, to answer your question, Emmett, no,
I didn't think it was funny, and no, I didn't have fun."

I was out of breath and almost panting by the time I finished.

He finally pulled up outside of my house, and he was staring
straight ahead. He wouldn't even turn to face me. *Fucking coward.*

"I'll marry you because I have to, and I don't want to make
my father's life any harder than it has to be, but don't think this
will be anything more than an obligation. Just know that I will
never love you again. You don't deserve it. Love is a weakness,
and I never intend on becoming weak again. This is all your fault.
I hate you for what you've done to me."

I was waiting for a reply, and when I finally concluded that

I wasn't getting one, I unbuckled the seatbelt and opened the door to leave.

I swear I heard a whispered, "I know," just as I was walking out of the car, but when I turned to look at him, I saw he hadn't even moved and was still staring straight ahead.

My eyes started filling with tears, and I turned right back around, walking up to my house and not looking back again. I refused to let him see me cry. He didn't deserve the sight of my tears.

I was about to close my front door when I heard my name being called, a door slamming, and feet slapping the pavement.

Shit. I forgot about Claire. I turned around and met her halfway.

When she reached me, she smiled and wrapped her arms around me. "I'm so proud of you, Rose."

I hugged her back and laughed. "For what?" I had no idea why she would be proud of me for that. I didn't like being mean. He deserved every bit of that lashing, but there was always a part of me that told me I needed to let go of the past and move forward.

"In all the years that we have been friends, I never understood why you never stood up for yourself when it came to the guys. Anytime they were mean or yelled at you, you always just sat there and took it. So, yeah, I'm proud of you."

She gave me one last squeeze before she let go. "I know you like to be alone, so I called Tommy to pick me up, but don't think I didn't hear you say something about being obligated to marry him. You owe me quite the explanation."

Tommy's car drove up the driveway, and she started walking away but stopped a few feet from the car and turned around. "I love you, Rose. Tell Sammy I said hi."

I gave her a slight nod and waved as they drove away.

When they were out of sight, I finally let the tears I'd been holding in fall and started my walk to the cemetery.

It was easier to love the dead. They couldn't be taken away from you a second time.

CHAPTER

Six

Emmett

Aﬀer leaving Rosie's house, I drove around the block and parked against the sidewalk. I didn't want to drive all the way home just in case Rose left to visit Sammy.

I turned on the interior lights to look at my knuckles, and sure enough, they were all split open, but it was all worth it. I wasn't about to let that piece of shit get off easy for touching what was mine.

At first, when I saw them dancing, I'd thought she was into it, so I forced myself to watch for a little bit because I deserved to feel the pain that came with seeing her with another guy. But when he grabbed her ass, I couldn't take it anymore. I usually tried not to be a violent person because I knew what I was capable of, and I didn't want to end up like my father, but I saw red.

I wanted so badly to grab her and show everyone she was mine, but the guilt of what I'd done to her stopped me from kissing her in front of hundreds of people. I was fueled by jealousy, and ready to stake my claim, but I couldn't allow her to think I was anything but an asshole, so instead, I did what was expected of me. I talked down to her and treated her like shit.

My thoughts were interrupted when I got a text from Lorenzo.

Lorenzo: She's at the cemetery.

Emmett: Be right there. I'd like a word with you also.

I threw the car into drive and headed toward the cemetery. It only took a minute because it was right down the street, but I had to park farther away, so she didn't hear my car.

I usually brought one of my others when I went to the cemetery, but I was riding in the Charger when I got a call from my bouncer at the club, saying Rosie was there and I didn't have time to switch them out.

Instead of going to my spot behind the tree, I walked up to Lorenzo first. "Why the fuck did you let her go into the club? And not only that, but you didn't think to tell me? I thought we had a deal," I barked at him.

Lorenzo had always been a little soft when it came to Rosie. If I didn't know any better, I would think he had a thing for her.

"Look, I'm sorry, but you know how it is. I felt bad. She'd been so sad all day, and I just wanted her to have fun. I was going to tell you, but I knew you would be busting in there to yank her out right away, so I figured one of your employees would tell you."

I was annoyed because he was right. They'd told me right away, but I wished I'd known beforehand. I could've doubled on security or told the bouncer not to let as many people in.

You couldn't trust anyone in this life. The club was packed with people, and anyone could've hurt her trying to get to the

49

Romanos. I didn't know what I would've done if something had happened to her.

"Next time, tell me," I snapped at him and walked to my spot, leaving him standing there.

I took a seat and leaned against the tree, listening to her words.

CHAPTER
Seven

Rose

Sixteen Years Old

I'D BEEN TRYING TO TALK TO EMMETT ALL DAY, AND I WAS starting to freak out because he wasn't answering me.

He was sent to the office for hitting Evan Davenport, and I hadn't seen or talked to him since.

Not knowing what else to do, I put on my shoes and left my room, ready to walk over to his house, but I stopped when I saw light coming from Sammy's bedroom.

I didn't know he was home. Maybe he knew where Emmett was.

"Sammy?" I lightly knocked on his bedroom door. "Are you in there?"

"Yeah, Bee, come in," he said through the door.

I walked in to see him sitting on his bed with his head in his hands. "Do you know where Emmett is? He hasn't been answering my calls or texts."

Sammy looked up at me with a frown. "His mom was killed today. Tommy and I were just over there, but he told us to leave and that he wants to be alone. I don't know what to do, Rosie. I've never seen him look so detached."

I didn't respond. Instead, I ran down the stairs, out of the house, across the street, and I didn't stop until I reached his door—which thankfully was unlocked.

I searched the whole house looking for him when I finally found Emmet sitting on a couch in his mom's library, staring at her chair.

"We were fighting this morning, and the last thing I said to her was that she was being a bitch. The last thing I would ever say to my mother, and I called her a bitch." He kicked the small table in front of him and put his head in his hands.

I walked further into the room and wrapped my arms around him from behind, pressing him against the back of the couch.

"He did it, you know." He paused for a minute. "My dad. He did it. I walked into the house because I didn't believe that she was actually gone, and I overheard him paying whoever it was that killed her."

I wished I could tell him that his father would never do such a thing, but Vincent Rossi was a disgusting human being, and I wouldn't have put it past him.

"I've been sitting here all day, hoping that it's not true and that any minute now, she's going to walk in and ask me about my day."

I pulled away, and when he still didn't move to get up, I took a seat on one of the chairs beside him.

I didn't notice the glass he had between his legs until it was flying across the room and smashing against the wall. "What am I going to do, Rosie? What am I supposed to do without her?

Live in this empty house and be reminded every day that I lost the most important person in my life?"

"You won't be alone. We're moving in with you," I heard from behind me.

I jerked my head to the side and saw Tommy, Claire, Lorenzo, and Sammy at the doorway with a bunch of bags around them.

I saw a bit of relief on Emmett's face, and although he was still sad, his breath came out a little easier.

That night, we laid blankets all over, and we all slept on the floor of Emmett's mom's library.

A few days later, we all stood around Emmett at the funeral, and I swear the whole city showed up to pay their respects to Emilia Montgomery.

I caught Emmett looking around a few times for his father, and my heart broke for him that Vincent hadn't shown up.

I knew a part of Emmett still craved his father's love and hoped that he wasn't the reason for Emilia's death, but another part of him wasn't surprised at all at what his father had done.

I think that was the day Emmett finally gave up on his father.

CHAPTER
Eight

Rose

I T HAD BEEN A MONTH AND A HALF SINCE MY FIGHT WITH Emmett.

I hadn't seen or spoken to him and tonight was our engagement party—funny how we were having an engagement party, and I didn't even have a ring.

I just wished I could sleep through this whole thing, but given that it was technically my party, my attendance was mandatory.

I was touching up my hair when there was a knock at the door. "Come in," I shouted to whoever it was.

My back was facing the door, so I looked up in the mirror and sighed in relief when I saw it was just Claire.

"Your dad looks hot today," Claire said with a smile and a wink.

I burst out laughing at her random remark. She must have been nervous or something. She word vomited when she was.

"Your hair looks good too," she added when I stopped laughing.

I had to admit my hair had come out really good. I used my small curling iron to make a bunch of small curls and put half of it into a high ponytail, leaving the rest down so I got the waterfall effect.

"Wait until you see my dress," I said as I walked into the closet to grab it.

It was a short white lace dress with a little slit on the thigh, definitely something Claire would've chosen herself.

I took the dress into my bathroom and quickly changed, zipping the back up as much as possible, but my arms didn't reach the whole way.

"Claire, do you mind coming in here and helping me zip it up?" I yelled from the bathroom.

She didn't answer, so I walked out of the bathroom with my head down and my hands behind me, still attempting to do it myself. "I can't get it the rest of the way up."

I hopped up and down, thinking it would help get the zipper up when a man's voice reached my ears, and I froze.

"Rose." Emmett's voice was so deep that hearing it instead of Claire's soft voice scared the fuck out of me. I damn near broke my neck from looking up so quick. I didn't even hear him knock.

"Emmett, you can't do that," I scolded him. "You scared the shit out of me. I literally almost peed."

"I brought you a ring to wear," he said sharply.

I looked down and saw a blue ring box with a bow wrapped around it in his hands.

I opened my hand to accept it, but he just placed it on the vanity and walked away like it wasn't a big deal.

How romantic. I hope he knew that he was justifying why I didn't want to do this.

I opened the ring box and almost fell over at what was inside. It was a white gold two karat cushion cut diamond ring with diamonds going around the band.

I wasn't surprised that he remembered the ring I'd always dreamed of having. It just pissed me off that he did this thoughtful thing and acted like he couldn't care less about me, not to mention he couldn't even be bothered to stick around and put it on my finger.

Looking at the time, I cursed when I saw it was 7:19. The party started at seven, and my father didn't care for tardiness.

I slipped the ring onto my finger and grabbed a metal hanger to help me zip the dress the rest of the way up.

I double-checked in the mirror to make sure I looked okay, and when I was satisfied, I started making my way downstairs to the party.

Walking down the steps, the first things I noticed were all the beautiful decorations and the table setups.

I wondered who planned this. It had to have been Claire since she knew what I liked, and this is exactly how I would want my engagement party to look. All white with succulents for centerpieces and greenery all around.

My father was at the bottom of the stairs, staring at me, looking impatient as ever, so I hurried down the rest of the steps before he could yell at me even more for my tardiness.

He grabbed my hand when I reached the bottom and pulled me in. "You're late," he said with annoyance. "I have many people to introduce to you, Rose. Where's Emmett?"

"I don't know. I figured he was down here," I responded with a shrug.

I saw someone walk by with a tray of champagne and quickly grabbed two glasses. I downed the first one and placed it back on the tray before she even walked away.

"When did you start drinking?" my father asked.

"Ever since you sold me to one of your enemies like a prized goat," I retorted with a mocking smile.

I felt him tense beside me, but he quickly shook it off and continued to pull me toward a group of men, some young, some old.

When we approached them, my father cleared his throat loudly. "Everyone, I'd like you to meet my daughter, Rose."

My father quickly introduced me to everyone and seeing as I was awful with names, they were quickly forgotten—not to mention they all looked the same to me. They must have been related or something, maybe a family from a different territory.

One of the men moved to my father's side and started whispering something in his ear, and my father nodded at him before turning to me. "I'll be right back. I just have to handle something really quickly."

Great.

Now I was stuck awkwardly standing here. I was about to give them an excuse and walk away when one of them—I think his name was Dimitri or something with a *D*—started to talk to me.

"So, you're Emmett Rossi's future bride, correct?" he asked.

I wanted to roll my eyes so bad because he obviously already knew that, but I'd promised I would be on my best behavior, so I settled for an eye twitch instead.

"Yes, I am. Our wedding is set for mid-November," I said with a polite smile.

I spotted Claire and Tommy standing in a corner, talking to Lorenzo and a girl who I assumed was Tommy's date. I was about to excuse myself to go to them when he cleared his throat.

"I wish I had known a pretty young thing such as yourself was up for grabs. I would've snatched you up." He moved to grab my wrist for added effect, but he'd barely gotten his hands on me before he was being thrown back a few feet.

Well, I'd found Emmett.

I didn't understand how he kept popping up out of nowhere and tossing people. I mean, don't get me wrong, he had perfect timing, but these mixed signals were giving me whiplash.

"If you try to touch my fiancée again, Demarco, I promise you it will be the last time you will be able to use your hands."

Demarco, that's what it was.

Ugh, see? Even his name sounded pushy.

Demarco quickly got up and straightened his suit, glaring at Emmett. Thankfully, all these people worked for my father. Otherwise, we could've had a serious fight on our hands.

Emmett grabbed me around my waist and pulled me away.

Normally, I wouldn't allow him to touch me, but considering how mad he looked, I'd rather not poke the bear.

He led me into a quiet corner and started whisper-yelling at me. "I can't leave you alone for five seconds without you getting into something." He managed to say all that and still kept his scowl in place. I'd be amazed at his ability to do that if it weren't for the fact that he was being annoying.

He acted as if I'd asked for this.

"It's not my fault. He came onto me, and I would've told him off if you hadn't thrown him first."

He just continued to stare at me with his scowl, so I let out an exasperated breath. "Look, I just want to get this party over with, so if you want to argue, we can do it later."

He gave me a tight nod and pulled me back toward the crowds of people.

Was this what my life had come to? Scheduled arguments?

I'd probably met over a hundred people tonight. I knew my house was big, but I had no idea it could even fit this many people comfortably.

I must admit, after meeting mostly everyone, a part of me was grateful to be marrying Emmett and not one of these guys. Most of them were extreme assholes and treated women like garbage.

Don't get me wrong, I knew Emmett was also an asshole but better the asshole you knew than the one you didn't.

For the most part, though, everyone else was being extremely friendly in congratulating Emmett and me on our engagement, so it wasn't as torturous as I would have thought.

Once my nerves settled, I found it actually felt kind of nice to have the gang back together so casually like this again, even though Sammy wasn't with us. I wasn't as sad as I'd thought I would be to be around everyone again without him. It felt almost peaceful in a way, but where there was peace, there was always chaos just waiting to be set free.

Emmett and I had been sitting at one of the tables talking to Claire, Tommy, and Tommy's date when I spotted Emmett's high school fling, Victoria Diego, coming toward us.

I guess somebody had let the chaos free.

I tugged on Emmett's arm to get his attention, and when he looked at me, I gave him the meanest glare and pointed in her direction.

"What the fuck is she doing here?"

His eyes followed my finger, and I heard him mutter a curse under his breath.

She walked up to our table and pulled up a chair to sit next to Emmett. If she sat any closer, she would have been on his lap.

I got a strong whiff of alcohol when she sat down, and Claire must have smelled it, too, because she started waving her hand in front of her nose.

By the looks of it, I was almost positive she'd gotten work done in the past couple of years. That nose was absolutely not real, and those tits definitely were not hers either. She was also wearing the shortest dress I'd ever seen. One sneeze, and her whole boob would be popping out.

"Emmett, why haven't you been answering any of my calls." She pouted at him.

You had to be kidding me.

Her?

Of all the people he could've been fucking, it had to be her? I'd be lying if I said this didn't sting a little. She gave me a lot of shit in high school, and he knew that. Even though I wasn't a meek little fifteen-year-old anymore, I still felt bad for young Rose, who went through daily verbal torture.

Looking around the table, I saw that everyone's jaws had dropped, even Tommy's date, who didn't know us from a hole in the wall. I watched as they all shifted their gazes to Emmett, waiting for his response, but Emmett had this annoying thing about him where if he didn't like your question, he just wouldn't answer. So, I guess I would just answer for him.

"Victoria," I said with the sweetest voice I could conjure, "I don't recall inviting you to Emmett's and my engagement party."

She looked away from Emmett and now noticed us all at the table, and after a few seconds, she smirked. "Well, if it isn't Claire, Tommy, and Rose. The gang's all here, but it looks like you're missing one, isn't that right, Rose? But who could it be? Oh, wait, I remember. Your brother! Didn't someone kill him? Well, it's for the best, really. I can't stand one of you, let alone two."

She knew damn well what happened to Sammy, and she knew better than to point her bitchiness in that direction. Hate me all you wanted, but don't say shit about my brother.

With that being said, I didn't feel bad for what I was about to do.

Without giving myself or anyone else any time to process what I was doing, I flew out of my chair and went right for her smug face.

Have fun finding some poor sap to buy you another nose, bitch.

She fell off her chair and slammed against the floor. I landed partially on her, so I quickly righted myself and continued to punch her over and over until I was being pulled back, but it didn't stop me from still trying to attack. I'd be damned if I would sit here and let her talk about my brother like that. Momma didn't raise no bitch, so you got to do what you got to do.

I managed to escape the hold I was in, and right when I got close, someone else was grabbing me when I was mid pounce. I turned to see who was holding me back, and of course, it was Emmett.

God forbid I ruin his chances of him getting his dick sucked.

I looked around to see if anybody saw, and sure enough, everyone was looking, including my father, who looked pissed. He'd probably heard her, or he was mad that I'd caused a scene—either way, I really didn't care.

Victoria was still on the floor, clutching her nose that was currently pouring blood and crying. A dark chuckle left me at the sight.

"I suggest you leave before I kick Emmett in the dick and come after you again." I turned to Emmett this time. "You can show your little friend out." I pried his hands off me and walked away with my head held high.

I felt my eyes filling up with tears and silently cursed myself for being an angry crier. I was trying to hold it in as much as I could, at least until I made it to my room, but I stopped at the top of the stairs when I heard my name being called.

I turned back to see who it was, and my eyes automatically searched for Emmett, hoping it was him, but when I finally found him, he was holding his hand out to help Victoria up.

I couldn't hear them, and Emmett's back was toward me, but I could see her nod, and then he pulled a napkin off the table, handing it to her so she could clean up some of the blood.

Shaking my head, I turned back around and continued to my room. How could he even stand to touch her after what she'd just said?

I got in my room and went directly into the bathroom to wash that bitch's blood off my hands. I was checking my dress to make sure I hadn't gotten blood on it when I heard my bedroom door open.

I really didn't want any visitors right now.

"If you're Claire, you can come in, but if you're not, then kindly fuck off."

"I've never been happier to be Claire in my life." She popped her head into the bathroom, and I started laughing. "So, Rocky, what do you say I force Tommy to buy us some alcohol, and we go to my house, get drunk, and forget our problems?"

She really knew the way to my heart. "I say, let me get out of this dress and pack a bag."

"How about you change, and I pack the bag—deal?"

"Deal."

I changed with lightning speed into a pair of short shorts and a tank top and walked to the stairs with Claire hot on my heels.

I stopped short going down the steps when I saw everyone was now gone except for my dad and a few staff members.

I put my head down when I reached my father. "Hey, sorry about the scene I caused, and I'm sorry you had to kick everyone out."

He let out a sigh and shook his head. "No worries. I heard what the girl said, and if it had been me, I probably would've done worse."

Well, that went a lot smoother than I'd thought it would go.

"Okay. I'm glad you're not mad, but I'm going to sleep at Claire's tonight. We're going to watch movies and hang out."

"Okay, but I want Lorenzo to go inside with you. I know Alessandro is away, and I don't want you two alone in the house."

Alessandro was Claire's father, who was also the mayor. He and my father had been friends for years. Although, I had no idea how deep their friendship went.

I'd always wondered if Mr. Rosario was involved in my father's business, and I knew better than to ask, but if I were honest, why would a mayor be good friends with a mafia boss if there wasn't anything sketchy going on?

"No problem. I'll go tell him." I grabbed Claire's hand and practically ran out of the front door.

Walking outside, I found Lorenzo in his car at the bottom of the driveway.

Poor Lorenzo. He always needed to be prepared, and on high alert, just in case I made a run for it or something. I hoped he got paid well because even I had to admit I was a handful.

I walked over to him and knocked on his window. "I'm going to Claire's for the night, but my father told me you have to be inside with me because her dad's away."

"Fine. Do you want to ride with me, or do you want to take your own car?" he asked.

"I'll ride with you because I was downing champagne earlier, and I don't like to drive like that." And, honestly, I was still coming off the adrenaline rush I'd gotten from beating up Victoria, so I would probably drive like a psychopath.

I threw all my stuff in the back, then hopped in the front with Lorenzo while Claire got in the back. I wondered what Lorenzo drove when he wasn't on Rose duty because, for some reason, I doubted he drove a Hyundai Sonata on the reg.

Now that I thought about it, though, when was he ever not on Rose duty?

We started driving away, and I was putting on my seat belt when Lorenzo slammed on the brakes and yelled at me, "What the fuck happened to your hands?"

I just continued putting my seat belt on and didn't answer.

Seeing my hesitation, Claire answered for me. "Long story short, some girl who used to try to bully Rose in high school and who we think is also fucking Emmett came to the party. The girl started talking shit about Sammy, and Rose beat that ass."

"Damn, I always miss all the action out here," he said, throwing his hands up.

"Well, tonight, you don't have to miss any more of the action because you will be inside with us. Speaking of action"—I turned around and looked at Claire—"did you text Tommy yet?"

She lifted her phone in the air. "Yeah, he said he'd be there in fifteen minutes."

"Woo-hoo, let's get this party started." I rolled my window down and screamed out of it for added effect.

We'd been in Claire's basement for a whole ten minutes, and in that time, Claire and I had already downed six shots of whiskey each. I guess it was safe to say we were feeling it. Fingers crossed that I didn't do anything reckless.

I was about to take another shot when I looked over at Lorenzo and noticed he was staring at the alcohol like he was in the desert, and it was the last bottle of water.

I knew he wouldn't drink with us because he thought my father would go crazy on him, but I wouldn't tell if he didn't.

"Lorenzo, take a shot with me, *please,*" I yelled.

"You know I can't do that, Rose. I'm supposed to be watching you." He shook his head at me.

"Funny you say that because, if my memory serves me correctly, I believe I saw you taking a body shot off that blonde chick at the club when we went, and you were supposed to be 'watching me,' so just take the fucking shot."

Lorenzo underestimated how observant I was sometimes.

He thought it over for a little bit and finally nodded. "Fine, but only one, and that's it."

Tommy finally took his tongue out of his date's throat long enough to turn in my direction. "Damn, Rose, I bet you could convince a priest to curse. Your manipulation skills are grade A. I kind of feel bad for Emmett."

Annnnnd there went my smile.

In Tommy's defense, he was super drunk, but still, ever since Emmett came back around, he was all everyone ever talked about.

I didn't want to sound like a brat but, does anybody remember the pain I went through when he left me? Was I just supposed to sit here and be happy now that I was marrying him? Just because the wound healed didn't mean there wasn't a scar. I just wanted to be able to go a full twenty-four hours without hearing his name.

At that, I poured everyone in the room two shots each, and I started handing them out. I'd spilled a decent amount, and my form was a little sloppy, but could you blame me?

Whiskey is some serious business.

I must've said that last part aloud because Claire agreed with me. "You're right. I'm definitely going to be hurting in the morning."

"Speaking of Emmett, where is my wonderful fiancé." I must have slurred my words because it took everyone a minute to understand what I was asking.

I lifted my left hand in the air and pointed to my ring to help speed up the understanding, and they all said "Ahh" at the same time, finally getting what I'd asked.

Out of everyone in the room, I was shocked that Lorenzo was the one to answer. "I believe he's taking care of some business at the club."

I felt like this was my last hoorah before I was married, so I slammed back another shot before I responded. "How would you know, Lorenzo?"

It wasn't like they'd talked from the time we'd left until now, and he'd been with us the whole time.

He must have been feeling a buzz because once he realized what I'd asked, his facial expression showed me that he'd slipped up.

I spotted his phone on the table in front of him, so as quickly as I could, I dove toward the table to grab it.

Once the phone was in my hands, I ran into the bathroom and locked the door so he couldn't come in and take it back.

His phone didn't have a password, so it unlocked easily. I opened the messaging app, and sure enough, Emmett's text thread was the first one.

7/3/19

Lorenzo: Going to the mall.

7/5/19

Lorenzo: No movement today.

7/7/19

Lorenzo: She's spending the night at Rosario's.

Lorenzo: I'm going with her. John's orders.

Emmett: Okay. Make sure she doesn't do anything stupid.

Lorenzo: Got it.

I felt so betrayed.

Lorenzo was supposed to be in my corner. Not his. Mine.

I opened the bathroom door and chucked his phone across the room at him while screaming, "*Traitor.*"

"Rose, I'm sorry. Please don't be like that," he begged.

He looked genuinely sorry but still. If he'd known I'd be mad, why'd he go along with it?

"Please don't be mad." Lorenzo gave me his puppy dog eyes, and I sighed.

"Fine. But don't talk to me for at least twenty-seven minutes or until I get over it, whichever comes first, got it?"

He nodded in response.

"Is Emmett's number still the same as before?" I asked.

Another nod.

He was really taking that no talking for twenty-seven minutes thing seriously. Good.

I pulled out my cell phone and dialed his number.

It rang twice before he picked up. "Rose." His voice rumbled through the phone.

"What's up, my dear *fiancé?*" I snarled.

"Are you drunk?" He didn't sound very happy.

Well, welcome to my world.

"Oh, me? I'm with my friends Robert and Marco. I just

finished jerking them off in the bathroom, and now we're on our way back to their place. They said something about a train, and you know I love rides."

I was about to go into detail when Claire ripped the phone away from me. "April fools," she said into the phone and hung up, throwing my phone across the room like it was a grenade about to detonate.

It was silent for a minute, and everyone was staring at my phone on the floor. Even Tommy stopped doing whatever the hell he'd been doing to look at my phone, and after about two minutes of silence, we all burst into a fit of hysterical laughter.

We ended up lying on the floor, still laughing about it ten minutes later when everyone abruptly stopped.

I opened my eyes to see what had happened, and that was when I found Emmett standing above me with his clothes soaked.

"Did you forget to take your clothes off for your shower?" I asked him, lifting myself off the floor.

He didn't think it was funny.

"Everyone out except for Rose. I would like a word with my future wife," he said, still not taking his eyes off me.

"You sure you want to talk right now? I'm very much intoxicated, and you barely like what comes out of my mouth on a regular day, so imagine what I'm going to say when I'm wasted?"

Everyone started walking out of the room until it was just me and Emmett left. He looked really pissed and I didn't really want to have this conversation with him right now. He was just going to ruin my buzz.

I tried walking away, but he just blocked my exit and growled.

"Rose, why do you have to keep testing my patience? You're making this harder than it needs to be. I'm trying to help you here."

Funny, last time I checked, I would've been fine living the rest of my life without him. I survived the aftermath of my twin's murder without him, so I'm sure at this point, I can do anything.

I saw him flinch, and I realized I must've said that aloud too. Dammit, I had to stop doing that. "I didn't mean to say that out loud."

"But you still meant it, right?" he asked.

Well, he had me on that one.

"What do you want me to say, Emmett? You know it's true, so let's not pretend we don't have a past, and to be honest, don't act like what I said hurt you. If you even gave a shit about me, you wouldn't have slept with Victoria Diego after everything I had to go through with her in high school."

"Not that it's any of your business, but I didn't sleep with her."

"Oh, yeah? So that whole time we were broken up, you never slept with anyone else?" I crossed my arms and tapped my foot.

"Don't ask questions you don't want the answer to, Rose." He scowled at me.

He obviously had. Otherwise, he would've told me.

"So, you have. Here I thought I was special. Maybe I should go even the score? Tommy probably hasn't started yet. I'm sure I can convince him to do me instead." I uncrossed my arms and pointed in the direction that everyone had left in.

I started to walk toward the steps when Emmett grabbed my arm, stopping me from going. I looked up at him once more, and I noticed his hard gaze had softened a bit.

"Rose, stop. It was a mistake. One that will not happen again. If you really want to know, there was only one girl, and that's it. Now please don't tell me yours because I don't want to know. It'll just make me angry."

"There's nothing to even tell. I haven't been with anyone

except for you, asshole." I poked a finger at his chest and crossed my arms.

It was true.

I could barely leave my room the first year, and the second year was spent trying to find a new normal—no time for dick. The thought of a random hookup or even dating had never even crossed my mind.

The slight grin on his face made me instantly regret telling him. Cocky bastard. I couldn't take it back now because he would know I was lying, so I blurted out the next best thing.

"Don't look so smug. There's still time," I snapped, and the grin slid right off his face. Score!

Rose: 1.

Emmett: 0.

The alcohol must have been wearing off because two things happened at once. I yawned, and I was hit with a wave of nausea.

"Um, Emmett? I think it's time for bed."

"Okay, I'll walk you to your room." He grabbed my hand, and we made our way up the stairs toward the guest rooms.

He stopped when we reached the top of the stairs. "Which room are you staying in?"

That was an excellent question because I had no idea. Emmett kicked everyone out before I'd had a chance to ask.

"Well, there are three possibilities, so the way I see it, I'm just going to open them all and see which one is empty."

I opened the first guest room on my right and saw that it was full of storage stuff. Definitely no room for me there.

When I opened the second guest bedroom door, I immediately regretted playing this game of "what's behind the door."

At first glance, I thought it was Tommy and his girl, but then I heard what sounded a lot like Claire's voice moaning Lorenzo's name, so I squinted my eyes to get a better look, and sure enough, there was Lorenzo pounding into my best friend.

I could've lived a happy life, not knowing what Lorenzo's naked ass looked like or Claire's boobs, but some things could never be unseen once you'd seen them, and this was one of those things.

Emmett must've seen them too because he looked at me with wide eyes when I turned around.

I didn't know what to say, so I closed the door and blurted out the first thing I could think of. "No room for me behind door number two. Onto door number three."

I scurried toward the next guest room, fingers crossed that I didn't see any more live porn, and I slowly opened the door, taking a cautious peek inside.

I was happy to report that the room was empty of all human life. I was a little scared that I would see Tommy's ass too, but we were clear.

Actually, I wouldn't mind seeing Tommy naked.

I heard Emmett growl behind me, and I realized I was thinking aloud again. *Oops.*

I walked inside the room and went straight to the attached bathroom.

I didn't know if it was the fact that I'd drunk so much or that I'd just seen Claire and Lorenzo going at it like rabbits, but whichever it was, I barely made it to the toilet before I started blowing chunks.

After five minutes of nonstop puking, I finally stopped and started to feel better.

It was when I flushed the toilet that I noticed Emmett was holding my hair up, and I couldn't help but comment with a laugh, "It's soon to be in sickness and in health, so you've passed part one. Congratulations."

He ignored my statement and lifted me to my feet. "You done? You need to lie down."

"Can you pass me the toothpaste and mouthwash first?" I reached out, and he placed the toothpaste in my hand and poured me a cup of mouth wash.

I put some toothpaste on my finger and did the best I could to clean my mouth, then I gargled the mouthwash and spat it into the sink. I wished I had my toothbrush, but it must have been in the room with Lorenzo and Claire, and I wasn't about to go back in there, so mouthwash and a finger brush would have to do.

I threw on some pajamas I found in one of the draws and slowly got into bed and did something I knew I was going to regret in the morning, but I was drunk, so right now, I was okay with it.

"Emmett, can you lay with me? Just for a little bit. Everything's spinning, and I won't fall asleep on my own," I asked, turning toward him.

He searched my face to make sure I wasn't joking. After a few seconds, he nodded and turned off the light.

I heard him taking his clothes off, and I tried to peek at him, but it was too dark. Why couldn't he have taken them off before he'd turned off the light? I'd been robbed of a good view.

He pulled the blankets up and slid into bed with me.

I replayed everything that had happened since I got to Claire's, and I couldn't help but smile.

Although it was small, I'd seen a piece of the old Emmett tonight.

Maybe it was because I was drunk and seeing things differently, or maybe he just thought it was okay for his mask to slip a little because he figured I wouldn't remember it in the morning, but either way, he wasn't as detached as he usually was.

If only it could always be this way, then maybe I could learn to forgive him. I wouldn't hold my breath, though. Tides changed, and Emmett came in waves.

I would never admit this to him—I hated even admitting it to myself—but having him next to me made me feel calm.

It wasn't long before my eyelids started getting heavy, and I was out like a light.

CHAPTER
Nine

Rose

I WAS NOT SO GRACEFULLY WOKEN UP BY CLAIRE'S LOUD mouth flying into the room, yelling, "Good morning, sunshine, how are you feeling?"

"Well, if I didn't already have a pounding headache, I would absolutely have one now." I rolled over and groaned.

She dove on top of me and slapped my ass. "Cry me a river. Get up and get downstairs. There's breakfast."

I was about to tell her that food was the last thing on my mind right now, but she was hopping off, skipping out of the door, and slamming it shut before I could even get my mouth open.

I wondered what had her in such a good mood when what I saw last night came back to me.

I looked over to see if Emmett was still there and noticed the side of the bed was perfectly made as if no one had ever been there. If it weren't for the fact I could still smell him, I would've thought it was all a dream.

I couldn't believe I asked him to sleep next to me and that I told him I hadn't had sex with anyone else.

Note to self: Do not drink excessively in the presence of one Emmett Rossi.

I rolled out of bed and started making my way downstairs. I didn't even bother changing. I just wanted to go home and regret every decision I'd made in the past twelve hours.

When I got to the kitchen, I spotted Lorenzo sitting at the breakfast bar. He looked up with a smile, and I gave him a dirty look.

Not only had he been giving Emmett updates on every single thing I'd been doing, but he also fucked my best friend.

I wasn't the type of person to get involved in other people's relationships, but Claire was my best friend, and no offense to Lorenzo, but he has slept with a lot of girls, and I didn't want to see my friend hurt.

I walked up to Claire, who was making pancakes and singing, and gave her a quick hug.

"I would love to stay for breakfast, but I feel like I ran full force into a brick wall, so I really need to go home, take a nap, and pop like three painkillers."

She nodded, and I gave her another hug before heading outside toward the car.

I waited until Lorenzo and I were parked at the house to unleash my anger so that I could look him in the eyes as I was flipping out. He had the car in park for point two seconds before I let the words free.

"You're skating on thin ice, Lorenzo Moretti." I snarled

He gave me a confused look and said, "What are you talking about?"

"Oh, I'll tell you what I'm talking about all right. Are you loyal to Emmett or me? You've been with me for six years, and you didn't think to let me know that Emmett was keeping tabs on me? How long has this been going on? And don't even think about lying."

He was looking down, so I couldn't see his facial expression and if I didn't have excellent hearing, I wouldn't have caught him say, "Since you guys broke up."

I couldn't help the obnoxious "*Ha*" that flew out of my mouth. "And you agreed to that? You're one of the people who saw me at my worst after what he did, and you still gave him the satisfaction of knowing my every move? I guess all I've ever been is a job to you. I thought we were actually friends, but friends don't betray each other like that."

I took a deep breath before I continued. "Not only did you do that, but you also slept with Claire. I'm sure it wasn't the first time, either. I'm also sure she doesn't know about the girls last week or the week before that or the two you had in your bed that one night. Do you see where I'm going with this, Lorenzo? Either man up and be with *just* her or don't be with her at all."

I opened the car door, slammed it shut, and walked to the house.

I couldn't look at him or let him respond because if he gave me his sad "I'm sorry" face, I was going to break and forgive him. I wanted him to sulk for at least day or two first.

He deserved worse, but Lorenzo had been with me through the hardest times in my life, and even though it was his job to stay with me, he always tried to cheer me up when I was sad and get my mind off things. He didn't have to do that, but I knew he wanted to.

The last thing I wanted was to lose someone else I was close to, but it still hurt that he'd kept me in the dark when he knew every little thing that had happened to me.

I walked up to my room, locked the door, and shut all the curtains. I considered writing a Do Not Disturb sign and taping it on the door, but my head was pounding, and I just wanted to go to sleep.

Thankfully, I was still in the pajamas I had found at Claire's, so I grabbed some painkillers, hopped into bed, and got comfy.

CHAPTER
Ten

Rose

I'D NEVER THOUGHT THAT PICKING OUT MY WEDDING DRESS would feel so depressing.

My mom looked like she was in pain, Claire looked disgusted, and Lorenzo looked uncomfortable.

At this point, I felt like I should just pick something so I could put everyone out of their misery, and we could all leave.

So far, I'd tried on a total of sixteen dresses, and none of them looked good on me.

I would have loved to try a mermaid-style dress, but the lady who worked here was pushing a ball gown.

I might just have to settle for something because the wedding was in a few months, and today was deadline day.

After showing everyone dress number seventeen, I was about to call it quits when I spotted a beautiful lace strapless mermaid dress on a mannequin. I walked up to it to get a better look and turned to the consultant. "Can I try this one on?"

She reluctantly nodded and started pulling it off the mannequin.

A few minutes later, she helped me out of the dress I had on, and I practically jumped into the new one.

Once I had it on, she clipped the back, and I looked in the mirror.

This was the one.

Everything about it was so beautiful, and I loved how it fitted my body.

Such a shame that the wedding was a lie.

I asked the consultant to get my mom so I could show her privately since she didn't talk much when other people were around.

I was still looking at myself in the mirror when Mom walked in, so I could see her eyes light up through the reflection. A single tear ran down her face, and I was stunned.

I'd never seen my mother cry in all my life. Sure, I'd heard her cry a few times through a doorway, but I'd never seen the tears, so I didn't know how I should react to this.

I grabbed a tissue from the table beside me and handed it to her cautiously.

"Mom?"

She took the tissue and dabbed her eyes. "You look so beautiful, Rose. I'm just so glad I get to be here to see you walk down the aisle. I know you don't want to marry him, and you feel like you have no choice, but your brother would be so happy to see you two together. He always said that if he had to pick someone for you, it would be Emmett."

Oh, now I understood the tears. She wished Sammy could be here. She'd been a shell since he'd been gone. So, hopefully, this was a step in the right direction to getting her back to how she used to be—or at least a sliver of how she used to be.

I stepped off the podium and gave her a hug. "I miss Sammy, too," I whispered.

She squeezed me and cried even harder.

After a few minutes, she pulled away and dabbed her eyes before looking up at me with a smile. "Okay, let's go show Claire."

I nodded and grabbed one last tissue for both of us before we made our way out.

Lorenzo spotted me first, and I heard a soft "Wow" come from him, which caused Claire to look up, and her jaw dropped.

"Damn, girl, you're looking like a ten. That dress is beautiful," Claire said with a wink.

I winked back and turned to the saleswoman. "I'll take this one."

CHAPTER
Eleven

Rose

THE NEXT COUPLE OF MONTHS WENT BY UNEVENTFULLY. I didn't see Emmett, and nobody talked about the upcoming wedding. I assumed it was out of fear that I might go crazy, but I told myself there was no sense in getting angry over something that was going to happen regardless of how I felt.

We only had two weeks until the wedding, and today was the third anniversary of Sammy's death. It was also my twenty-first birthday, but I refused to celebrate without Sammy, not that anybody objected anyway.

I'd always been told that it got easier with time, but as the years went on, I still felt so empty.

I woke up this morning with a heavy heart, and I had to force myself out of bed to start the day.

When I was younger, I used to look forward to my birthday every year, but now, I dreaded it.

I was dressed and walking down the hall when I heard Mom

in her room, crying again. In the beginning, I never used to hear her cry, but I think it was getting to be too much for her as time passed. I wanted to comfort her, but the last time I'd tried, she wouldn't open the door, and it made me sadder than I was before I'd knocked.

Dad's office was a little farther down the hall, and I had already smelled the alcohol the second I'd opened my bedroom door. He'd been drinking a lot more lately, and I hoped it didn't get out of control.

I knew Mom blamed him for Sammy's death, and in a way, I did too, but I knew nobody blamed him more than he did himself. He got shot that night, too, only his wasn't fatal.

I hated how fucked up everything was. We went from a perfectly happy family to this with the snap of a finger.

I wouldn't have wished this life on my worst enemy.

I got two of Sammy's favorite cupcakes from the bakery down the street like I'd done every year, only this year, I had Lorenzo's help because last year, I'd dropped one of the cupcakes when I was trying to light it, and I had a full-blown panic attack.

I sat down at Sammy's grave and took one of the cupcakes and the plate from Lorenzo. He lit both of them, gave me a nod, and went back to the car, giving me some privacy.

"Happy birthday, Sammy. We are twenty-one today, can you believe it? We can legally drink now! Not that it matters. We were going to parties and getting wasted since we were fifteen." I chuckled lightly.

I started silently singing happy birthday, and when I finished,

I blew out the candles and started eating my cupcake. I stopped halfway and put it back down on the plate.

I held it together as much as I could, but with each year passing, I felt like it was getting harder, and I couldn't hold it in anymore.

"I really fucking miss you, Sammy. Everything's a mess. I can't tell you the last time I heard Mom's laugh, Dad's drinking himself to death, and I'm so damn lonely. It's so hard to keep going when the only thing I want to do is give up. You always told me everyone has a purpose, and I've tried, but I just can't find mine." Pushing everything aside, I lay down on the grass. "I don't know how much more I can take. I'm just so sad, Sammy."

I lay there until the sun started to set, and then I remembered that Lorenzo was with me and was probably starving, so I should get going.

Sitting up, I kissed my fingers and touched them to the headstone. "I've got to go, Sammy. Until next time. I love you."

CHAPTER
Twelve

Emmett

PULLING UP TO THE ROMANO HOUSE, I RECHECKED THE text I got from John this morning to make sure I had the time right.

John Romano: My office. 7 p.m.

It was the day before the wedding, so I was a little nervous about this meeting. I hoped he hadn't changed his mind—the last thing I needed was for John to break our agreement.

I got out of my car and knocked on the front door. A guard answered and silently ushered me toward John's office.

I knocked, but when there was no response, I slowly opened the door.

It was only open a crack, and I could already smell the bourbon. The man clearly had an issue with alcohol. Every time I saw him, he was either drunk or on his way there.

John's back was toward me, and he was staring at a family photo behind his desk.

"This was taken exactly a week before he was killed.

Everyone looks so happy." He turned around to look at me and took a seat at his desk. "Take a seat."

His eyes were so bloodshot that I wondered when the last time he'd slept was and seeing all the empty bottles of alcohol on his desk, I also wondered when was the last time he'd had some water.

Taking a seat, I waited for him to start.

In the time I'd known John, I'd never had a conversation alone with him. So I was thoroughly confused as to why he'd asked to talk to me, especially considering I'd been sitting here for a whole two minutes, and he'd been staring at me the whole time, not saying anything.

I opened my mouth to ask him why he'd asked me to come here when I was cut off.

"I'm very aware of your past with my daughter, and I'm also aware of the fact that she hates you right now."

Right to the point, I see. Dig the knife in deeper, why don't you.

"With that being said, I know she will fall in love with you again, and I need you to know that if you break her heart a second time, I will kill you."

Well, shit.

Not only did the man pay attention, but he actually cared. Who would've thought?

Now, I'd never disliked John in any way, but just out of curiosity, I asked, "No disrespect, Mr. Romano, but why did you agree to our marriage?"

Staring without speaking must have been his thing because he was doing it again—full-blown eye contact, and he wasn't even blinking, just watching me.

After another couple of minutes passed, and I was about to get up and walk away when he cleared his throat. "I once let my need for power become so important to me that I lost my son to a war that I caused all because of money. I would give everything to get my son back. The money means nothing to me now, but it's too late.

"My wife hasn't told me she loved me in three years. My daughter hasn't been able to look me in the eyes since Sammy's funeral. Every night, I sit outside my bedroom and listen to my wife cry herself to sleep. Rose hates this life, and I know you do too. If anyone can get out of it, it's you, and I want you to do that. I can't go back and save my son, but I can save my daughter."

I nodded my head in understanding, and we both stood up.

"I know you love Rose and that you felt you had no choice but to leave her, but you should be the one to tell her why you left before she finds out through someone else."

With one last look at him, I gave him a nod and walked out of his office without saying a word.

I'd always seen John Romano as a selfish man, who didn't care about anything except money and power, but today, he'd gained a little more respect from me.

As far as Rosie went, I couldn't tell her.

I'd already broken her heart once. It was best if I didn't do it a second time.

CHAPTER
Thirteen

Rose

I T HADN'T HIT ME YET THAT I WAS GETTING MARRIED TODAY. I was just numb.

Even as I sat in front of the mirror while some random lady did my hair, it still just felt like any other day.

Claire kept tiptoeing around me as if I was going to snap at any minute, but I guess I could understand that, considering I hadn't said more than two words at a time for hours.

The lady finished my hair and told me it was time to put on my dress.

I slipped it on and walked up to the floor-to-ceiling mirror.

I stood there for a little while just looking at myself, and all I could think of was that it was such a shame that I was wasting this beautiful wedding dress on a man who didn't even like me, let alone love me.

In the weeks leading up to this day, I'd imagined myself being sad and crying any time I thought about what I was being subjected to, all the dreams I was forced to throw away, but the only emotion I felt in this very moment was anger.

I guess that was why the only person allowed in this room with me was Claire.

"It's time. Let's start heading down and taking our places." The wedding planner cheered.

Her name was Julia or something like that, but either way, she'd planned my whole wedding, and this was the first time I was meeting her.

I made my way to my father and slipped my arm through his, ready to make my way down the aisle.

"You look beautiful, principessa," my father said with a smile.

When I gave him no response, he continued, "I'm sorry if—"

"Don't even bother," I cut him off. "This is your doing. I will never forgive you for making me do this. Spare me your words because nothing you say will change how I feel."

I hated being mean to my father. I tried to be grateful for him being so kind to me growing up, but he took my brother away from me, and now he was giving me away. I couldn't forgive him for that, I believed him when he said he had no choice, but it didn't make it sting any less.

He gave me a nod, and I was about to apologize for being so mean because I knew my head was just all over the place today, and I was taking it out on him, but before I had the chance, the doors opened, and the music started to play.

"You ready?" my father asked.

"No, but let's go before I try to make a run for it."

I looked forward, and there was Emmett at the end of the aisle, looking straight at me with a blank face. I didn't know what I'd expected of him today, but he wasn't even pretending to be happy.

When we reached the end of the aisle, I looked up at Emmett and let out a breath.

"Dearly beloved, we are gathered here today…"

Here goes nothing.

The ceremony went by in a blur. The vows were short and clipped, and the kiss was as quick as a blink of an eye.

I felt like a robot going through its daily routine without any emotion, not once letting a smile appear on my face at my own wedding, a day that was supposed to be one of the happiest in my life.

When it was time for the reception, I was being pulled in all different directions, meeting so many different people, greeting them, and thanking everyone for coming.

Ironic how I grew up going to weddings just like this, watching the brides fake nice with these same people, but I could always see the sadness in their eyes.

The grooms never cared. They knew they'd be able to continue with their lives the same as they had been, the only difference being they had a wife at home to act as a personal maid.

I always told myself that I would never be that girl who married someone she didn't love, but now look at me.

I didn't have much of a choice, though, did I?

Just another bride, sitting on a shelf like a fucking trophy.

I was sitting at my table next to Emmett when I felt the first tear fall, but I wiped it away just as quickly as it appeared.

"I need to use the bathroom," I said to no one. I quickly got up, gathered the bottom of my dress, and left the room searching for a bathroom.

When I spotted it, I hurried inside and locked the door behind me. Walking up to the sink, I looked at my reflection in the mirror.

I'd never been good at knowing what to do with my emotions. I'd normally just shut down and pretend everything was okay, but lately, there had been so much going on, and it was getting overwhelming.

All my emotions were building, and I couldn't handle it. It was as if there was a bomb in my head ticking, and the timer was running out.

So, I did what I told myself I wouldn't do anymore after Sammy had died. I let the darkness consume me and allowed the anger trapped within me to be set free.

It only took a few seconds before everything went black.

Emmett

She'd been in the bathroom for eleven minutes now.

Usually, I wouldn't be worried, but I saw the look in her eyes before she walked off, so that was what had me walking out of the ballroom and toward the bathroom to make sure everything was okay.

I got to the first bathroom and tried opening the door, but it was locked. I was about to walk away, thinking she wasn't in there when I heard her scream inside.

Springing into action, I kicked the door down, ready to kill whoever had her screaming like that. The first thing I saw was Rose crouched down in the corner of the bathroom, crying and her hands bleeding.

I opened every stall, ready to strangle the person responsible for harming her, but there was nobody in here except for her.

She didn't look up at me when I sat next to her and slid her into my lap. She just stayed bundled up in the fetal position, hyperventilating from crying so much.

I pulled her hands away from her face and forced her to look at me so she could calm down and tell me what was wrong, but the words got stuck the minute she looked up at me, and I saw how sad she looked.

Seeing her like this absolutely killed me. I hated looking into her eyes and seeing so much pain and anger.

I let go of her hands and held her until she stopped crying, and her breathing returned to normal.

A few minutes later, she moved out of my lap and looked around the room, seeing everything around her scattered and destroyed.

"I always wondered when I would break again." She laughed. "It's ironic how the room matches how I feel inside." She turned and looked at me, fresh tears running down her face.

"I hate that you got to see me like this. Not because I'm embarrassed, but because you don't deserve my emotions, and you don't get to help me through a hard time. You left me. I needed you, and you left me. You were always my constant. I always thought that no matter what happened in my life, it would be okay because I still had you, but boy, was I wrong. You took my already broken heart, and you shattered it.

"You want to know what the worst part of it all is? No matter how bad you hurt me, a part of me still hopes that you could be the one for me again. That one day you'll love me like you used to, and we can live happily ever after just like you promised, but the ending to our first story sucked, and this sequel is even worse."

She walked to the door and turned to look at me again. "You've changed. You're so cold, and I don't know if you've even realized it. I honestly feel bad for you. Every time I look at you, all I see are those black eyes looking back at me, and I wonder if you will ever go back to who you used to be."

She forced out a dark laugh and shook her head. "Did you know that two weeks ago was the third anniversary of Sammy's death? Three years ago, my other half died, but so did you. The only difference is you're standing right in front of me, but I have no idea who you are."

And then she walked out.

I didn't bother to follow.

She was right. I was different. And as much as I would have loved to be together again, to be happy and blissfully married, it was impossible. The things I had done to her were unforgivable.

Rose

Walking back to the ballroom, I wiped my tears one last time and went in search of Claire so we could go back to the room where she could help me clean up the blood. Thankfully, I had yet to get any on my dress—it would be a disgrace to stain such a beauty.

I spotted her on the dance floor with Tommy, Lorenzo, and Tommy's date.

Could I just point out that I had never seen Tommy with the same woman more than once? I seriously couldn't wait for him to find the right girl who knocked him on his ass.

I was almost to them when I was abruptly cut off by el diablo—I mean Vincent. "I've been looking all over for you, Rose."

At this point, I didn't even bother to fake a smile with him. I knew he just became my father-in-law, but after my breakdown, I was exhausted and just wanted to get cleaned up.

"Well, you've found me, but if you'll excuse me, I really have to talk to somebody."

I tried to walk around him, but he grabbed my shoulder and yanked me back. I wasn't in the mood for this shit right now, so I quickly shook him off and gave him the meanest glare I could.

"I'll do you a favor and not tell my father or Emmett about what you just did, but don't expect for me to be so generous next time."

I was surprised when he smiled and stepped out of my way. I'd expected more of a fight from Vincent, but maybe the gods had decided to spare me for once.

I'd always hated how Vincent looked at me, but he at least had never put his hands on me, until now, of course. It was as if some twisted part of him thought he had control over me now that I was married to his son.

Yeah, not today, Satan.

I felt some more blood trickle down from the cut on my hand and hit the floor, so I pushed Vincent to the back of my mind and continued on my way to Claire.

I walked up behind Claire, trying to hide my hands so nobody would see, but I must not have been as stealthy as

I'd thought because Lorenzo turned and zeroed in on all the blood, and I could see the murder in his eyes.

I smiled at Lorenzo and shook my head, hoping he got the message that I was okay and not to cause a scene, but I saw him reach behind his back for his gun, so I quickly mouthed, "It's okay."

He just looked at me for a bit with his hand still on his gun. I guess he wasn't content with my answer because he rushed to my side.

"I had a breakdown and broke some stuff, cutting my hand in the process. It's fine—I'm fine. I just need Claire to help me up in my room. Just give me five minutes."

Finally, he gave me a tight nod and put his hand back to his side.

Why must my life be surrounded by overprotective men?

I went behind Claire and tapped her shoulder. "It's me. I need your help with something." I didn't give her time to respond and just pulled her to the exit.

"May I ask what we're doing and where we are going?" she asked with her back still to me.

I waited till we were in the elevator to show her my hands. "I blacked out and broke a bunch of shit, so I need to get this cleaned up."

She looked down at all the blood and blanched. "Holy shit, Rose, are you fucking crazy? That's a lot of blood. What if you need stitches?"

"Don't be so dramatic. There would be a lot more blood if I needed stitches, so let's throw some alcohol on this shit and get this night over with."

"That's the spirit," she said as she rolled her eyes at me.

We got to the room and cleaned up my hands in record

time, then headed back. Hopefully, we were quick enough that no one noticed our absence.

We were almost back to the ballroom, but as we got closer, I noticed people were leaving.

I mean, I wasn't complaining, but I was curious as to why considering it was still early.

Turning to Claire, I gave her a confused look, but then I started to worry that something had happened. "You go look for Tommy, and I'll look for Emmett." She nodded, and we went in opposite directions.

I searched the room for Emmett and found him across the room, speaking to the governor and his wife.

I'd spoken with them earlier when they'd congratulated me. I'd thought they were invited because of my father, but now I wondered how Emmett knew them.

I started moving toward them to find out what was going on when I saw a woman waltz right up to Emmett, grab both of his arms, and start kissing his neck.

Oh, wow, what a bitch.

Usually, I wasn't so judgmental, but the way she was touching him looked so casual like she'd done it many times.

Then it all made sense. She must be the girl he'd slept with.

As if she could hear my thoughts, she looked my way with a sneer and pressed her body closer to his.

It took me a minute, but I finally recognized her.

She was the governor's daughter, Bethany Castellanos.

I saw the appeal. As much as I hated to admit it, she was beautiful—long blonde hair, porcelain skin, and a nice body.

Her hand started traveling from his shoulders down his body, all while Emmett was still in conversation with her parents.

He wasn't even attempting to push her away.

Did they have any morals at all?

I decided I no longer wanted to watch some girl grab all over my husband, so I looked for Lorenzo instead.

This night was starting to feel more like a high school prom and less like a wedding—so much damn drama.

I found Lorenzo leaning against one of the entrances, talking to Tommy and Claire so I turned and made my way to them instead.

"Lorenzo, why is everyone leaving?" I asked when I reached him.

"No idea. One minute everyone was dancing, and the next, Emmett comes in and tells everyone to go home."

Well, I didn't expect that one.

"Do you know where I'm staying tonight? I'd like to go to bed."

He gave me a puzzled look as if I were asking him a trick question. "Emmett's house. I'll go grab him so that we can go."

He looked at Emmett, and I could tell he knew who Emmett was talking to because he stopped and quickly stepped in front of me to block them from my view.

I gave Lorenzo the fakest smile I could. "Don't worry. I don't want to interrupt him. If you don't want to take me, I'm sure Tommy here will be glad to."

Lorenzo's eyes went wide, and he shook his head.

Poor Lorenzo. He was always stuck in the middle of everyone's drama. "No. It's okay, I'll take you," he said with a sigh.

Yeah, I was tired of this shit too. "Perfect, I'll follow you out."

Lorenzo pulled up to the biggest house I'd ever seen. I thought I lived in a huge house before, but this one was like a mansion.

Lorenzo parked the car in front of what I assumed was the front entrance and got out. He rounded the hood of the car to open the passenger door for me, but the car was so low that I couldn't seem to lift myself out in this dress.

He held his hands out for me to grab so I could pull myself out, but it was harder than it looked.

After my third attempt at pulling myself out, Lorenzo finally gave me some help and tugged me out. He then grabbed the back of my dress while I grabbed the front, and we made our way up the steps to the big-ass mansion house.

I was surprised there wasn't another entrance for this place that led directly into the house because there must have been about a hundred steps leading up to the door.

Lorenzo cleared his throat from behind me. "Sorry about the walk. I don't have the sensor in my car that allows us to go into the parking garage, so we have to go through the front."

I guess he was a mind reader now.

He followed me up the steps, and by the time we reached the top, I was out of breath.

I made a mental note to start going to the gym or maybe take up running again because I was out of shape.

Lorenzo opened the door to a long hallway that was completely bare, which led to a huge sitting room. The sitting room seemed to be the center of everything, with a massive open space above.

Looking around, I found that Emmett's house was just as I'd expected it would be. It lacked the warm feeling you get when you walked into a home. His house was cold and barely looked lived in.

There were so many closed doors and staircases connected to the sitting area that I almost regretted coming here without Emmett so he could show me around. But then I remembered how the governor's daughter was all over him, and how he didn't do a thing to stop it, so I didn't regret it anymore.

I hated how I was actually hurt by seeing them together.

"Lorenzo?" I called out.

He popped his head out from behind the wall of what looked like the kitchen. "Yeah?"

"Do you think I'm an idiot for going through with this?"

He walked out of the kitchen with a frown and pulled me in for a long hug.

Letting me go, he grabbed my dress and led me down a small hallway that opened up to a large living room with a gigantic fireplace.

He walked me to the couch and motioned for me to sit. "Why would you think that?" he asked me as he sat down.

"I don't know, Lorenzo." I sighed. "I just don't want to be the stay-at-home wife whose husband is always out working or sleeping with his mistresses. It's our wedding night, and he already has another girl all over him. I just feel stupid."

Great, now he was giving me the sad eyes.

"Rosie, you are the smartest and strongest girl I know, and if I ever hear you say some shit like that about yourself again, I'm going to burn your favorite shirt."

Well damn. Hit me where it hurts, why don't you.

"If any man thinks you're going to be that type of woman, they are not only a dumbass but sadly mistaken. Now, I'm going to put on a funny movie, and we are going to watch it and laugh, okay?"

"Okay," I said with a nod and lay down on the couch.

Lorenzo put on *The Sitter*, and by the middle of the movie, we were both in tears from laughing so hard.

I must have fallen asleep because the next thing I knew, hands were wrapping around me and lifting me from the couch.

I leaned into Lorenzo as he lifted me off the couch. "Sorry that I fell asleep before the ending, Enzo. It's been a long day."

I opened my eyes a tiny bit, and I saw Lorenzo still asleep on the couch. I almost started freaking out, but then I took a deep breath and realized it was Emmett—he'd used the same cologne ever since I could remember.

I contemplated telling him to let me down, but after today, I didn't have the energy, so I just let myself fall back asleep.

CHAPTER
Fourteen

Rose

I WOKE UP ALONE AND STILL IN MY WEDDING DRESS.

At least I could say I got my money's worth, although it was kind of depressing. Normally, people woke up naked after their wedding night, definitely not still in their dress.

I tried to undo the back of the dress to take it off, but my arms didn't reach.

I was starting to think my arms were getting shorter. I'd never had these problems before.

I looked into the bathroom and the walk-in closet for Emmett so he could help me, but with no luck, I bunched up my dress and just made my way to the kitchen. I had no idea how to get there, but I was sure I would find it eventually.

After two dead ends and one spin, I found Lorenzo at the kitchen counter, reading a newspaper.

"What are you doing here?" I asked.

He lowered the newspaper and frowned. "What do you mean, what am I doing here? I'm always with you."

"You're still my guard?"

"Yes, why wouldn't I be?"

I'd been worried that when I married Emmett, Lorenzo would no longer be my guard because he was one of my father's men, and considering I was now a Rossi, I'd just assumed I would get one of Vincent's men. I wasn't complaining, though. Vincent was such a terrible person that I could only imagine what his men were like.

"Where's Emmett?" I asked, changing the subject.

"He had an early meeting this morning, so he left about an hour ago."

"What does he even do for work? Do you know when he will be back? I need help getting out of this dress."

"No idea. All I know is that he has an office, and maybe he'll be back in a few hours. I can call him if you want."

"Don't worry about it. Can you just unhook the back for me?"

He gave me a horrified look in response and fumbled for his phone. He put the phone to his ear—calling who I assumed was Emmett—and stuttered, "Yeah, she needs help getting out of her dress."

I would have paid good money to find out what Emmett had said or done to have Lorenzo so scared of touching me.

Lorenzo hung up and let out a long breath. "Emmett will be here in five to help you."

I rolled my eyes at him. "Okay, Lorenzo. I don't understand why you can't do it since it's only a little bit of bare back. Are you forgetting I saw your pasty white ass full moon style when you were fucking my friend?"

"Fair point, but I value my fingers, thank you very much," he said back with a wink.

"Whatever. Tell my *husband* I'll be in the closet."

Exactly five minutes later—I couldn't stand the punctual bastard—I was sitting in the closet, playing on my phone, when Emmett walked in.

I looked up and forced a smile. "Good morning, darling. How was your meeting?" He wanted a trophy wife, he was going to get a trophy wife.

He rolled his eyes at me, ignoring my question. "My father wants us to attend dinner with him and his wife on Sunday."

Fake or not, my smile was instantly wiped off my face.

"In New York?" I groaned.

I'd never been comfortable around Vincent, but in New York, I would be in his territory, which was ten times worse.

"Yes. Is that a problem, *darling*?"

I put my game face back on. "Nope." I made sure to pop the *P*. "That's perfectly fine."

Emmett went behind me and unhooked the back of my dress, zipping it down enough for me to reach it. "Anything else you need?"

"That's it, thanks."

"I'll be seeing you later tonight then." He stopped at the door. "If you need anything, there's a room downstairs near the front door with a few security guys, and Lorenzo will be with you all day."

"Everyone but you, dear husband," I said when he walked away.

I spent the next few days looking around and getting used to my surroundings.

On the third day of me living with Emmett, I went into the

kitchen, where I found Lorenzo talking into his cell phone. He looked up at me and quickly hung up.

"Emmett will be late tonight. He told me to tell you to eat dinner without him."

Surprise, surprise.

I rolled my eyes and started taking out all the stuff I needed to make lasagna.

"He couldn't tell me that himself?" Lorenzo gave me a shrug, so I continued, "Can you hand me my phone please?"

Lorenzo got up from the counter and handed me my phone while looking at all the ingredients. "What are you making?"

"Lasagna," I said while opening my text app and typing a message to Emmett. "Don't worry. I'm making enough for everyone."

Rose: Busy with the Governors daughter?

I put my phone down and started prepping the food. Once I finished, I checked my phone to see if he'd answered, but there was nothing. I knew I was being petty, but we'd never talked about how she was all over him at the wedding, and to be honest, I was still hurt about it.

When the lasagna was done, I took out six plates and put a generous portion on the guys' plates and a smaller one for me.

Lorenzo already had a fork in hand, sitting at the island, ready to eat.

"Not yet. You have to help me take these to the security guys." I slid two plates to him, and I picked up the other two. "Take those to the guys outside, and I'll give these to the guys inside."

The door to the security room was open, so I walked in and handed the guys their plates. When they saw what it was, I could almost see the drool coming out of their mouths.

I'd made dinner for everyone every night. The first night,

they were confused and thought it was some kind of test, but after I assured them it was not, they dove right in. I tried to get them to eat with me in the dining room, but they politely declined, so it had just been Lorenzo and me eating dinner together every night.

I hadn't spoken much to the guys outside because they were at the gate, which Lorenzo didn't allow me to go near—you would think I was in danger or something. I'd had more freedom at my parents' house.

It was the same guys every day—Dom and Damon outside, and Raphael and Lucas inside.

Raphael was quieter, the "no speaking without being spoken to" type, but Lucas was the funny, talking all the time type. He was always making jokes about how wonderful I was and how he wanted to run away with me. I never took it seriously, though, and the way he looked at Raphael told me that I wasn't the one he wanted to run away with.

Lucas took a huge bite and looked up at me with a moan. "You're my favorite wet dream—beautiful and knows how to cook. Marry me, Rose?" We both started laughing, but then his laughter abruptly stopped.

"You won't be able to if you're dead," came from behind me.

I spun around to find Emmett behind me with his black eyes and emotionless face. If it weren't for his threat, you would never be able to tell he was annoyed.

Lucas looked at me, then Emmett with wide eyes and started to stutter.

I got on my tiptoes so I could get Emmett's attention and gave him a death glare. "He was joking. You should take the stick out of your ass and try it sometime."

He ignored me and continued to stare at Lucas. "You will

not talk to my wife like that again, or you'll find yourself with a bullet in your kneecap very quickly."

I swear I wanted to choke the life out of him. "At least he doesn't rub his hands all over my body. I guess you're the only one allowed to be hit on and groped. Noted."

I left the security room and went into the kitchen to grab my lasagna. Lorenzo had already finished his first piece and was grabbing another slice.

Not wanting to drag Lorenzo into yet another situation, I took a seat in the dining room alone and was about to take a bite when Emmett walked into the room, looking pissed.

This was the first time he was showing emotion, so I must have really made him angry. Good.

"I don't appreciate you talking to me like that in front of my employees, Rose. As far as Beth goes, I told you not to ask questions you won't like the answer to."

"Well, maybe you shouldn't flaunt your little girlfriend in front of my face. She was all over you at our *wedding*, and you didn't stop her. How would you feel if I was walking around with a guy that I fucked? Letting him touch me and kiss my neck. I'm sure you would love it."

"What did you expect, for me to never have sex again? We broke up, Rose. It's been three years," he said with a huff.

That made me laugh. "You're right, Emmett. I'm so sorry for thinking you could wait a little longer before sticking your dick in someone else."

He closed his eyes and took a deep breath, calming down before opening them back up and continuing, "You're right, I shouldn't have allowed her to do that at the wedding, and I won't let it happen again. I have not slept with anyone for a few months, and I swear I will not cheat on you."

I was stunned silent for a little bit. I definitely wasn't expecting that response.

"Okay." That made me feel a little better. It still didn't help the sting, but there was nothing I could do about it now.

He gave me a tired look. "I don't want to fight with you. I'm not trying to be stuck in a miserable marriage, so how about we drop it and try to get along?"

I hated that he was right. We should make the most of this instead of being at each other's throats. "Fine." I sighed. "I made lasagna if you're hungry."

I hoped Lorenzo had already eaten it all.

It had been a whole week of me living here, and I'd successfully walked through Emmett's entire mansion.

It was beautiful and judging by the family portraits hung up in one of the studies, this house must've been in Emmett's mother's family for generations.

Emmett had never told me about this house, though judging by the big sign that said Montgomery Mining next to all the family portraits, I was starting to feel that there were a lot of things about Emmett that I didn't know.

I was in the library when Emmett came home, and he found me sitting against one of the shelves on the second floor. "I had a bet with Lorenzo that you would find the library in the first week of you being here. He said you wouldn't find it unless someone told you there was one, so he owes me a hundred bucks."

I had to admit, ever since our kind of truce, he'd been surprisingly pleasant, still *very* distant and cold toward me, but at least now he didn't act as if my presence repulsed him anymore. He still didn't smile or laugh, but at this point, I'd take what I could get.

I looked up at him and laughed. "Well, you're barely here, so I got bored. Besides, how else am I supposed to find out all the things you've kept from me? I have tons of questions. Why didn't you ever tell me your mom was rich?"

"I had no idea she was until my eighteenth birthday. My mother's lawyer called me and told me I needed to come in for a meeting about my inheritance. At first, I didn't believe him because I'd never heard of him before, and I didn't know my mother even had a lawyer, but then I got to thinking about how Mom never talked about her family, so I thought, 'screw it' and went to meet him a year later.

"He told me that my mother's parents were the owners of Montgomery Mining and that the company had been in the family for years. He then went on to tell me he had strict orders to not talk to my father about Mom's secret will and that I had inherited everything.

"After he told me all that, I laughed and said, 'You must have the wrong guy because my mother never mentioned any of this when she was alive.' But then he started pulling out papers, and right there on the bottom was my mom's signature. Mom always had a perfect signature and wrote her e's a different way, so I knew everything the lawyer had told me was true. I always assumed that Mom took Dad's abuse to keep us safe and because she needed the money, but I'll never understand why she didn't just take me and run away, why she would let Dad constantly beat her down when she didn't even need him."

Emmett never spoke of his mother. When we were

together, I always tried pushing him to talk, but he would just lash out and walk away.

I'd always felt bad for Emmett. He only ever had his mom, and before she'd died, he started working a lot and saving up money so that his mom could cut ties with his father. He must've been devastated to find out years later that she could've run away with Emmett if she'd wanted to. Money was never the issue.

Things can always be different. You can always hope for a different outcome, but even though you know it's not possible, it doesn't make it hurt any less.

"I'm sorry, Emmett."

He gave me a shrug, looking down at the floor. "It's fine. It's in the past."

Not wanting to push him too much about his mother, I quickly changed the subject. "So, what do you want to do for dinner? I can make pizza."

"Pineapple?" He lifted his head and quirked an eyebrow.

"Still your favorite, huh? How about half?"

"Deal."

In the kitchen, I started grabbing all the ingredients I needed while Emmett grabbed me an apron and some drinks.

I slipped on the apron, and Emmett started mixing different drinks and juices into a glass for me. When he was done with my drink, he poured himself a very generous shot of whiskey.

He handed me the final product of mine, and I had to say, the man could make a mean drink. Whatever he put in this made it delicious but dangerous. It tasted like juice, and I was already halfway done with it before I'd even made the pizza dough.

After about an hour and two drinks later, I put a pizza

with half-pineapple and half-pepperoni and two pizzas with everything into the oven.

We were both sitting on the counter with our drinks when I turned to Emmett. "I'll never admit this again, so don't ask me to, but I'm glad it was you. I'm still hurt by what you did to me, but if I was going to be forced into marrying someone, I'm glad it was you."

When he didn't answer, I looked up to find him staring at me with a smirk on his face.

Here he goes, getting cocky.

I dipped my fingers into the bag of flour beside me, grabbed a pinch, and flicked it in his face.

He gave me a shocked expression and shook his head at me. "Oh, you're going to regret that one, Rosie."

I didn't have time to dwell on the fact that this was the first time he had called me Rosie in so long because he made a move to grab me. I dodged his hands, hopped off the counter, and with lightning speed, I booked it out of the kitchen, laughing my ass off.

I didn't make it far because the next thing I knew, I was being lifted off my feet and spun.

"You think you're funny, Rosie, but you wait until I get you back," he said as he carried me back to the kitchen and sat me on the counter, caging me in with his arms.

And that was when I spotted the egg in his hands.

I reached for his ticklish spot so I could run, but it was too late because, in the same moment, the egg cracked and ran down my hair and face.

I guess he wanted to play dirty, so I checked my surroundings and found the butter right next to one of my hands. Not only was it spreadable butter, but it was super soft from being out of the fridge. He was making this too easy for me.

I grabbed a handful of butter and slowly smeared it down his face. The look of pure confusion he gave me had me laughing so hard that tears mixed with egg whites were running down my face.

"Where the fuck did you get butter?" He looked around and found it behind me. "Shit."

I was still on the counter, caged in and laughing when he looked at me. "You think you're so funny, don't you?"

I stopped laughing, and he leaned into me like he was about to kiss me but stopped right before our lips met, waiting for permission.

I gave him a small nod, and he pushed forward. I was thankful I was sitting on the counter because his mouth still had the ability to make me weak.

I gripped his face and was about to deepen the kiss when he pulled back to look at me. He opened his mouth to say something but stopped when my wrist caught his eye. I looked at my tattooed wrist and realized this was the first time he'd seen it.

"I got it after Sammy died. He gave me a birthday card before he left just in case he wasn't home when I woke up. It's the last thing he wrote to me, so I found someone who could replicate it and got it tattooed. Anytime I feel sad or lost, it helps me remember."

He pulled away as if I were on fire and looked in every direction except for the one I was in.

"We should check on the pizza and see if it's done."

I wanted to ask him what happened for him to pull away from me like that but decided against it—one step forward, two steps back.

I looked into the oven and pulled the pizzas out, deciding

they were ready. I put them on the counter and yelled for the guys, telling them their pizza was ready.

I'd lost my appetite, so instead of eating, I walked up to the room where I'd been sleeping.

As I lay in bed, I reflected on the past couple of days and how, after our truce, things had started getting a little better between us, but he'd just flipped the switch again, and it felt like we were back to square one.

CHAPTER
Fifteen

Rose

TODAY WAS SUNDAY, WHICH MEANT WE WERE HAVING dinner at my lovely father-in-law's house.

Emmett and I hadn't really spoken since he freaked out about our kiss, but maybe our mutual dislike for his father would bring us back to neutral ground.

The only plus side to going to Vincent's house was that I got to ride in a helicopter to New York. The views were amazing, and we landed just as the sun was setting.

The excitement was short-lived though because now we were pulling up to the devil's castle, and I had to play nice.

And it was a castle. The place was huge.

With all the windows in the front, it kind of reminded me of Alcatraz, and it looked ancient too, so I wouldn't have been surprised if this place was haunted.

Vincent's house fit him well, though. Dark, creepy, and a splash of arrogance.

"Please, just don't provoke him," Emmett said while he

knocked on the door. "The quicker we get to eat, the quicker we can leave."

I wanted to argue that my attitude toward him was almost uncontrollable, that he brought the worst out of me, and it wasn't my fault his father was the equivalent of el diablo, but Emmett already looked stressed, so I just kept my mouth shut.

"Fine by me. Let's get this over with."

The massive doors were pulled open, and a woman greeted us with a tight smile. "Good evening, Emmett. It's good to see you. It's been so long."

I didn't recognize her, so I wondered how they knew each other. She looked young, and I had to admit that she was very beautiful.

Emmett gave her a nod. "You as well, Stephanie."

Oh, okay, now it made sense. It was Vincent's wife. I thought I was going to finally meet her at the wedding, but I guess Vincent doesn't allow his wife to leave the house unless absolutely necessary—or at least that's what Lorenzo told me when I asked.

I'd always wondered what she would look like, and this was nothing like what I'd pictured.

Vincent must have had a type because Stephanie and Emilia could have passed for sisters—petite, dirty blonde hair, light brown eyes, and a button nose. I didn't know why, but for some reason, I'd pictured her as being the complete opposite.

He mustn't have really cared for her because he let her open the door. Growing up, my father always had a rule that only a guard or himself was to open the door in case an enemy was on the other side.

Now that I thought about it, I didn't even think Vincent had any guards. I'd thought it was weird when we pulled up, and there wasn't a gate. I just figured all the security would be inside the house, but when I looked around, there were no men in sight. Meanwhile, the number of men my father and Emmett had around could have made up two different soccer teams.

Stephanie closed the door behind us and faced her body to Emmett, but her eyes pointed to the floor. "Your father would like for you to meet him in his office."

Emmett nodded and turned to me. "Are you going to be okay?" He was probably nervous that I was going to plant a bomb or something.

I gave him a reassuring smile and nodded. "Yeah, I'll just hang out with Stephanie."

He nodded once more and squeezed my shoulder before walking away.

I turned back to Stephanie, and even though she was still looking down, I smiled at her. "You have a beautiful home. I'm Rose, by the way. It's nice to meet you."

It was true. Although the outside resembled a haunted prison, the interior décor was beautiful. A replica *David of Michelangelo* statue greeted you in the entry with double staircases leading to the upstairs, and art lined the walls. It screamed wealth, but I expected nothing less from Vincent.

Stephanie's gaze stayed glued to the floor of the entryway. "If you'll follow me, I can show you around a bit," she said softly.

She tilted her head up for a second and was so busy trying to avoid eye contact that she accidentally tripped on my foot when she went to step around me.

I stuck my arm out to catch her so she didn't fall, but my angle was wrong, which caused us to drop to the ground like a sack of potatoes.

I jumped up, then bent down and stuck my hand out to help her up when she flinched. I quickly pulled my hand back to my side and frowned.

From what Emmett told me, Stephanie had been married to

Vincent for a little over twenty years, since she was only sixteen, and judging by the way she flinched when I got close to her, he most definitely wasn't a loving husband.

She must have snapped out of whatever state she'd put herself in when she thought I was going to hit her because she quickly got up and started apologizing.

After the fourth time saying she was sorry, I gently placed my arms on either side of her and forced her to look at me. That was when I noticed the frantic look in her eyes. "You don't have to apologize, Stephanie. It was an accident. It's okay."

She nodded in return, and I felt her relax a little under my grip.

I hooked my arm in hers and walked in the direction she was headed before she tripped. "How about that tour?"

By the end of the tour, I'd seen every part of the house except for the basement, which Stephanie said was Vincent's space, which was off-limits.

I didn't have any time to ask questions because the next thing I knew, I was being pulled toward Emmett's younger half-siblings' bedroom to meet them. Stephanie had four children with Vincent—ten-year-old Romeo, eight-year-old Natalia, six-year-old Jacob, and three-year-old Gianna.

We were all in Gianna's room while Gianna sat on my lap, Jacob talked to me about all his friends at school, Natalia showed me her dolls, and Romeo sat quietly beside me.

Emmett's siblings were the sweetest despite the kind of person their father was. They were apprehensive at first, but once

115

they warmed up to me, they were all over me, talking a mile a minute.

Gianna got up from my lap to get her favorite doll Lucy to change her outfit because she wanted Lucy and me to match.

I helped Gianna put the outfit on and looked at all the other doll clothes she had. "I love all your doll clothes. I wish I had them in my size," I said to Gianna, and her eyes lit up.

"I can ask miss Emily to make some for you. She's the one who makes our dolls' clothes for us," Natalia said, trying to pull me up.

Stephanie got up and turned to her kids. "Let's go downstairs and get ready for dinner. Your father should be ready." Natalia frowned and dropped my hand, then we all got up and made way to the dining room.

We'd just sat down when Emmett and his father appeared from one of the hallways. Emmett sat in the seat beside me while Vincent sat across from him.

"Rose, it's so good to see you," Vincent said, looking me over while licking his lips.

I'd wondered when I married Emmett if Vincent would stop being an inappropriate creep toward me. I guess I got my answer. I really wanted to tell him where to go and how to get there, but I'd promised Emmett I would play nice, so I gave him a fake smile and forced out, "You also, Mr. Rossi."

He looked me up and down one last time before he focused on Emmett. "This is the first time you're seeing your sister Gianna. Gianna, say hello to your brother Emmett."

Gianna was on the other side of me, so she moved to hide behind my arm.

"Gianna, do not be rude. Say hello to your brother. Now," Vincent barked at her.

When she still didn't say it, Vincent punched the table, and everyone jumped. I looked at Gianna and saw tears starting to build.

He opened his mouth, probably to yell at her, and I sat up in my seat a little, ready to give him a piece of my mind if he did, but Emmett cut him off instead. "She's shy, and she doesn't know me, so it's not a big deal." He turned to Gianna. "Hello, I'm Emmett. It's nice to meet you."

Gianna gave Emmett a shy smile while Vincent gave him a dirty look and turned to his wife. "Go get the food. I'm hungry."

Stephanie jumped up and practically ran to the kitchen.

"So, Emmett, how's business going?" Vincent asked with a mocking expression.

"Good. Profits have been high lately, and I have a good system going."

I quickly got bored with their conversation and decided to help Stephanie in the kitchen. "I'm going to give Stephanie a hand," I whispered in Emmett's ear before walking away.

The minute I got into the kitchen, I saw the panic on Stephanie's face. "What's wrong? Is everything okay? What happened?" I asked quickly.

She jumped when she heard my voice. "Oh, Rose, it's nothing. I just left the meatballs in the oven for a little too long, and they're a little dry. Vincent will be upset, but it's okay." She gave me a sad smile.

I nodded, and without giving it a second thought, I picked up the pan of meatballs and dropped it on the floor, causing the glass to shatter and sauce to go everywhere. I instantly heard chairs being pushed back and stomping feet getting louder.

I looked over at Stephanie's shocked face and gave her a wink just as Emmett came barreling into the room with Vincent close behind him. Maybe I was sticking my nose where it didn't belong, but I couldn't sit back and watch him treat his family like shit.

"You okay? What happened?" Emmett asked, looking around.

"I'm so clumsy," I said with a small laugh. "I was just smelling Stephanie's meatballs, and the pan slipped right out of my fingers."

I grabbed some paper towels and started cleaning up the mess while Stephanie started picking up the glass.

Vincent snorted. "Well, I guess I will have to do without my favorite dish now, won't I?"

I gave him a big fake smile and shrugged. "Stephanie and I will finish cleaning up this mess and will be right out with the rest of it!"

Vincent gave one last snort and walked out of the kitchen. He probably didn't believe me, but he didn't call me on it.

Emmett just looked at me, laughed, and followed his father back to the dining room.

When they were out of sight, Stephanie dropped everything she had and hugged me. "Thank you for that. You have no idea what you just did for me."

I dropped the paper towel in my hand and hugged her back. "Anytime. Vincent's an asshole. If you don't mind me asking, though, why are you still with him?"

She dropped down to the floor and continued to collect glass. I figured she wasn't going to answer my question until I heard her start to speak in an almost inaudible whisper. "Besides the fact that he'll probably kill me, I married him when I was sixteen years old. My father signed off on the marriage so he could get in good with the Family. I never finished high school, so without him, I have nothing. He wasn't as bad when I was younger. Other women told me horror stories of marriage and their husbands, so I just kept telling myself that it could be worse. He would sometimes push me around and call me names, but he didn't beat me until years later.

"I was twenty-five when I first met Emmett. He'd just turned eight and had come to New York to stay for a week for the first time. Vincent had just had the basement redone to be sound-proof. Emmett was running through the house chasing me and accidentally smashed into the basement door, making a small dent. I told him it was no big deal, but when Vincent got home, he dragged Emmett downstairs and beat him so bad the poor boy stayed down there for two days because he couldn't walk up the steps. I tried stopping Vincent, but he slapped me and locked me in our bedroom. From that day forward, I vowed I would never have Vincent's children, so I convinced one of the maids to sneak in birth control for me. I never really wanted to sleep with Vincent, but I was always taught that sex was a chore, so I never fought him.

"Vincent always questioned why I wasn't getting preg-nant. He would tell me I was broken, but I didn't mind because I would never want my children to go through what Emmett went through, so I took the verbal lashings he would give me. It wasn't until one day he came home early, and I had forgotten to hide the birth control, and he found it. That was the first time Vincent ever beat me. He kept me locked in a room in the base-ment for four months, forcing himself on me until I got preg-nant. I dream of one day taking my children and running away, but Vincent's resources would never allow that."

Looking into Stephanie's eyes, I saw years of pain behind them, and it broke my heart. Tears started to build in my eyes, and she wiped them away.

"Don't cry for me, Rose. This is the life I was given, and I've come to terms with it. You've done so much for me already, and I thank you. Let's get back out there. I'm sure you're hungry."

The rest of dinner went by in a fog.

I couldn't stop replaying the story Stephanie had told me. I couldn't even look at Vincent because, to be honest, I might have taken my steak knife, jumped over the table, and stabbed him in the dick.

I was staring off into space, still thinking, when I felt Emmett shake my arm. "Right, Rose?"

"Right," I said back without even knowing what I was responding to.

He pulled me up out of the chair and turned to everyone. "Well, we have to get going. I have a few things to do at the office. It was a pleasure."

I gave my goodbyes to Emmett's siblings, and when I reached Stephanie, I pulled out the piece of paper I'd swiped from the kitchen earlier in the night, and I shoved it in her pocket while I hugged her.

"If you ever need anything, don't be afraid to call," I whispered in her ear before I pulled away.

She nodded, and I was walking to the door when Vincent grabbed my arm and pulled me in for a hug.

"Can't wait to see you again, Rose," he said into my ear.

I tried pulling away, but he tightened his grip on me. I was about to bite the fucker, but Emmett's voice stopped me.

"You can let go of my wife now, Father." He had the don't fuck with me tone, and I had to admit, I was kind of turned on by it.

Who was I kidding, though? Anything Emmett did turned me on. He may have hurt me, but that didn't make him any less attractive.

Vincent let go of me, and I practically ran to Emmett's side. "Let's get out of here," I said while pulling him toward the car.

I must've fallen asleep on the ride back because I woke up in Emmett's arms, being carried into the house.

"Careful, big guy," I responded in a sleepy voice. "You're going to catch a cough carrying this smoke show."

He let out a light chuckle. "You still got those lame-ass jokes, huh?"

"Oh, shut it. You loved my lame-ass jokes."

We got to my room, and he laid me down on the bed. "You're right. Good night, Rosie."

"Wait," I rushed out. "Happy birthday, Emmett." I grabbed his face, pulled him down toward me, and kissed him on the cheek.

We both froze when my lips met his face.

I quickly pulled away and punched his arm, trying to turn our interaction into something more friendly. I didn't know where that came from. I wasn't even thinking—it was so instinctual. I blame it on me still being half-asleep.

His eyebrows jumped in surprise. "You remembered?"

"Of course, I did. I thought that's why we were going to dinner at your father's, but when there was no cake, I got very confused."

"I doubt my father even knows how old I am, let alone when my birthday is."

"Well, it's okay. He's a douche. I actually have something for you." I got up and not so gracefully walked into my closet. When I found the photo album, I pulled it out and handed it to him. "It's kinda corny, but I got it for you for your eighteenth birthday, and I totally forgot about it until I was packing up my stuff for the move and found it hidden in the depths of my closet."

He opened it up and started looking inside.

"It has pictures of all of us inside, even Tommy and Claire, but it's mostly you, Sammy, and me from when we were younger up until I was sixteen. I recently added a few more of you and Sammy from before he died. Anyway, I hope you like it."

It had made me sad when I found a picture of Emmett, Sammy, and me from a couple of days before Sammy died. They both had an arm around me, and we were all smiling from ear to ear at the camera. The girl I was back then was almost unrecognizable.

In that picture, I didn't have a care in the world. If you had told me back then that the following week I would lose everything important to me, I would've laughed in your face and punched you for good measure.

"Thank you." He walked out of the room with the album in his hands, and I didn't see him for the rest of the night or the next day.

CHAPTER
Sixteen

Rose

Seventeen Years Old

S AMMY HAD BEEN BANGING ON MY DOOR FOR THE PAST five minutes, yelling at me to hurry up, or we were going to be late to Emmett and Tommy's graduation party. But Emmett liked my hair when it was curled, and my hair was thick as hell, so it took a while for me to perfect it.

"Give me a minute, Sammy. I'm almost done," I yelled through my door.

"If you're not done in the next five minutes, I'm leaving without you, Bee."

I released the last curl, unplugged the curling iron, and took a look in the mirror to make sure I looked good. I threw the door open just as Sammy was going in for another loud-ass knock, and I had to dodge his fist because it was still coming down.

"Perfection is not easy, Sammy. You would understand if

you had more than two inches of hair." I stuck my tongue out at him, and he laughed.

"Oh, cry me a river. Let's go before Emmett gets mad."

Thankfully, Emmett lived across the street, so it only took a minute to get there.

Walking in, I looked around at all the people and let out a huff. It was going to take me forever to find Emmett.

After fifteen minutes and two laps around the main floor, I gave up searching for him and made my way outside for some fresh air. Once outside, I noticed someone lying in the grass, and when I moved a little closer, I saw that it was Emmett, so I popped down beside him.

"I just spent a solid amount of time looking for you inside. I should've known you were out here. You've never liked crowds like that."

It was quiet for a while. He didn't speak, and neither did I, the two of us just content with looking up at the dark sky.

"I used to be bad at math when I was younger, so Mom and I used to come out here and practice every day after school. My dad used to tell me that school isn't a priority and that I should stop being such a pussy. I guess a part of me knew that Dad wouldn't show up today because he never cared about school, but it really fucking sucks that my mom couldn't be there for me because I know she would've been the first person there."

I rolled over and laid my head on his chest. I tried to find the words to make him feel better, but nothing I said would change how he felt.

"Don't get me wrong," he continued, "I despise my dad, but it still sucked seeing everyone with their parents, and I didn't have anyone. I guess what I'm trying to say is, I miss my mom."

With my head still lying on him, I started running my fingers up and down his chest and stomach.

"Tell me a lie, Rosie," he whispered.

I lifted my head and smirked at him. "I told you it would grow on you."

"I'm waiting," he said, rolling his eyes.

I lay back down and searched my head for a lie. "Okay, fine, I didn't kiss Tommy when we were in sixth grade."

He pushed up onto his elbows and nearly knocked me off him. "I'm going to kick his ass. He promised he would never touch you!"

Now it was my turn to roll my eyes. "Oh, get over it. We were ten."

"A promise is a promise," he growled at me. "Tell me a truth."

It took me a minute to build up the courage to respond. "I want to marry you."

He grabbed my hand and pulled us up so that we were standing. "Why don't we just do it?"

"Do what?" I asked. "Get married?"

"Yeah."

The stars must have been getting to his head. "I'm still seventeen."

"So, we wait," he said. "We wait until your eighteenth birthday, and we just do it."

I was about to tell him he was crazy, but when I thought about it, I'd loved Emmett for forever, and I didn't want to be with anyone else, so why not?

"Okay, let's do it," I told him. "Pinky promise."

He held out his pinky, and I wrapped mine around his. He pulled me in and threw his arms around me, lifting me in the air and swinging me around.

"I love you, Rosie."

"I love you more, Emmett."

CHAPTER
Seventeen

Rose

EMMETT AND I HAD BEEN MARRIED FOR ALMOST TWO months now, and in that time, all I'd done was sit in the library and read.

I swear I was slowly losing my mind, so I'd made the executive decision to go to Emmett's office and demand he give me work to do. I'd taken a few online courses after I graduated high school, but I'd never put them to good use.

Walking into my closet, I decided on something professional but with a dash of sexy. A dark gray pencil skirt that went up to my waist, teamed with a long-sleeve white blouse with a deep V to show off the girls and some red bottoms. I put my hair half up and half down with curls, showing off my single dark blue highlight, and I was ready to go.

I went into the kitchen for Lorenzo and found him sitting at the island, eating a sandwich. I swear all the man did was eat.

When he spotted me, he stopped chewing and slowly put the sandwich down.

"I need you to take me to Emmett's office today."

Lorenzo looked at me the way he did whenever he thought I was saying something crazy and laughed. "You're joking, right?"

"Do I look like I'm kidding?" I said while pointing to my outfit. "Why don't we skip the part where I blackmail you, and you just take me?"

He thought about it for a moment but ended up grabbing his keys, mumbling something about me being nuts.

Yeah, yeah, tell me something I don't know, Moretti.

Walking into Montgomery Mining, I turned to Lorenzo. "Which way is his office?"

"No idea. I've never been here before." When I gave him a look, he continued, "I'm too busy making sure no one kills you all day. When would I have time to come here?"

"Well, when do you fit fucking my best friend into your schedule?" I lifted my eyebrow at him.

He rolled his eyes at me. "You're going to have to get over that one, Rose."

"I will when you marry her," I said with a big smile as I walked up to the blonde at the front desk.

She had on one of those headsets you saw receptionists on TV wearing. "May I help you?" the blonde asked without looking up.

"I'm looking for Emmett Rossi."

Blondie glanced up from her desk, looked me up and down, and scoffed. "And you are?"

I looked over at Lorenzo and gave him a look that said, "What's this chick's problem?" and he shrugged his shoulders.

"His wife," I said, turning back toward her.

She rolled her eyes in response and laughed. "Your name?" she asked as if she didn't believe me.

If she asked me one more question, I was going to throttle her.

"Rose Rossi," I said with a smile. I hated how the first time I used my married name had to be to this girl.

She started pressing buttons on her phone to call, I assumed, Emmett, and she transformed into a shy little schoolgirl. "Hi, Emmett. So sorry to bother you, but there's a Rose here to see you. I can send her away if you're busy."

Now it was my turn to roll my eyes. Was she even supposed to be using his first name? I looked around her desk to see if I could find her name, and sure enough, there it was, front and center. Tiffany Ellis.

She hung up, and a minute later, Emmett was walking down a hall toward me.

I started walking to meet him halfway, but I stopped short when Tiffany got in between us—literally.

Now, I wasn't proud of what I was about to do, but in my defense, she was rude first. I'd never been the type of person to back down from a battle, and if blondie wanted to play, then I'd play.

"Hey, baby," I said, walking around her. I wrapped my arms around him, and he placed his hands on my hips. I didn't give him time to talk because I was already up on my tiptoes, kissing him. Knowing everyone was watching, I deepened the kiss to get my point across.

It was when he kissed me back, though, that my knees

started to weaken, and he wrapped his arms around me to keep me from falling.

I was about to start pawing at his clothes when I heard someone clear their throat, snapping me back to reality. I quickly pulled away, looking up at him a little dazed.

To add a dramatic effect, I took my thumb and rubbed my lipstick off Emmett's mouth. "I missed you so much."

He narrowed his eyes at me, probably trying to figure out why I was acting like this. "Why don't we go into my office."

I turned to Tiffany and smiled at her, laughing when I saw that her jaw had dropped. I winked at her and smiled. "Thanks for your help."

She let out a huff and marched back behind her desk.

Set and match.

Emmett grabbed my hand and led me to his office. "Don't take this the wrong way, but what was that?"

"It seems your secretary has a little crush on you," I said when we walked in, and he closed the door.

He took a seat behind his desk and gave me a smirk.

"Oh, please. Wipe that look off your face. As if you wouldn't do the same." I muttered the last part.

His look turned dark, and I rolled my eyes. I would never understand why men were the way they were.

"Okay, well, I came here for a reason, so can we get to it?" I said, crossing my arms.

"Of course, let's get to it then." He leaned back in his chair and folded his hands in his lap.

"I'm sick of being home all day, and I was hoping you could give me something to work on. Maybe I can help you out here with paperwork and stuff, or I could replace your receptionist." I said the last part with a lowered voice and another eye roll.

"You want to work for me?" He cocked his eyebrow up like he was skeptical of what I was asking.

"Well, yes. I'm bored as hell in that big-ass house."

He nodded and sat there, contemplating my request for a little while. "Well, I guess I have a few things around here I need help with. I've never had an assistant." He shrugged.

"Perfect. I can start right now."

CHAPTER
Eighteen

Rose

WORKING WITH EMMETT ACTUALLY WASN'T BAD IF you looked over the fact that a good portion of the people working for him were female, and they all threw themselves at him constantly.

Although I did enjoy watching him reject all of them and hit them with, "Have you met my wife, Rose?"

I knew he was just being respectful of me, and I tried not to let it go to my head, but I'd be lying if I said hearing that didn't make my smile a little brighter. My smile almost always faltered when we got home, though, and he acted as if I wasn't even there.

Claire was coming over today, and I couldn't wait for the workday to be over so I could have some fun instead of shutting myself in the library all night.

I was in my bedroom, getting dressed when my door flew open, and Claire came barreling in with a bottle in each hand.

"The fucking party is here," she screamed, throwing her arms in the air.

I was shirtless, but that didn't stop me from screaming and running to my best friend to hug her. I regretted not wearing a shirt, though, when the next thing I knew, Emmett and Lucas came charging in, guns drawn.

Claire rolled her eyes and put the bottle down, pulling out two shot glasses. "Have you never seen a pair of chicks who've missed each other?"

Emmett gave us a dirty look and noticed I had no shirt on, so he quickly shoved Lucas out of the room. "Would you put a fucking shirt on?" he growled at me.

I grabbed my shirt and took my sweet time throwing it on. "Well, maybe you shouldn't barge into people's rooms unannounced."

He huffed at me before walking out and slamming the door behind him.

"What's up his ass?" Claire asked, cracking open a bottle of rum.

"It's probably been a while, so maybe he needs to get laid." I shrugged.

Claire lifted an eyebrow and stopped pouring the shots. "And are you going to help him fix that problem?"

"Yeah, right. We kissed twice, and every time we get close, he can't get away from me fast enough."

She handed me the shot, and we clinked the glasses together before throwing the drink back.

"I'll never understand men," Claire said, pouring another shot and handing it to me.

"I'll drink to that."

I was buzzing hard now. So hard that my brain lost the battle with my vagina, and I was currently on my way to Emmett's room. I slowly opened his bedroom door and saw him asleep on his back. I walked in and quietly closed the door behind me, tiptoeing up to him. Thankfully, the blinds were open, and the moon was giving off just enough light that I could see his body.

I hopped on the bed, straddling him, and his eyes flew open, but he relaxed when he saw that it was just me.

"What are you doing?" he asked, rubbing an eye.

I could feel his dick starting to harden, so I started rolling my hips to speed up the process.

"Rose," he growled, "What are you doing?"

"*Shhh*." I took my shirt off and ran a finger across his bottom lip. "Just close your eyes and relax." I lifted my body and pulled down his sweatpants, letting his perfect eight inches spring free.

"We really shouldn't be doing this, Rose." He was trying to deny me, but his eyes were starting to get wild.

I pushed my shorts to the side and started lowering myself onto his dick. I was so wet that I didn't even need the foreplay. I was sure he would slide in with little effort.

He reached up, probably trying to stop me from going down any further, but I dropped down before he could get a good grip on me, allowing him to sink all the way inside of me.

I had to admit, it did hurt a little, probably because I hadn't had sex in over three years, but after a few seconds, I started to stretch around him.

"Rose, we should stop—"

"Just relax," I said, cutting him off. "It's just sex, Emmett. It's not a big deal."

His eyes thinned, and he grabbed my hips, flipping us over so that he was on top. "Fine," he barked at me. "You want just sex? I'll give you just sex."

He put a pillow under my back and started pounding into me fast and hard, going deeper with each thrust.

I started moaning louder when I felt myself getting close.

He put a nipple into his mouth and rubbed the other one, and that was what threw me over the edge completely. He finished right after, and neither of us spoke or moved.

I looked up into his eyes, and I watched as they slowly got darker.

He opened his mouth, but by the look in his eyes, I already knew what he was going to say, so I shook my head at him.

Not wanting to hear him tell me it couldn't happen again and that it was a mistake, I slid out from under him, threw my shirt back on, and left.

The next morning, he left for work without me.

He didn't come home that night. Or the night after that.

It was a full week before I saw him again.

I knew I was the one who initially walked away, but I was also trying to save myself from being hurt.

When he finally came back, he fed me a bullshit excuse, not once looking me in the eye. He didn't even give me a chance to respond before he walked away once again.

It was easy to be the one to walk away. You don't have to watch what you were leaving behind.

CHAPTER
Nineteen

Rose

FOR THE PAST COUPLE OF SUNDAYS, I'D BEEN ABLE TO get myself out of going to dinner at Emmett's father's house, but this Sunday marked six months that Emmett and I had been married, and I guess Vincent had something to tell us.

Walking up to the door, Emmett gave me the "be on your best behavior" look just as the door opened, and Gianna ran into my arms, knocking me back a few steps.

"Rosie, you came back," she said, jumping up for me to pick her up.

I lifted her, and she gave me a big hug.

"I missed you," she said, squeezing me with her tiny hands.

I hugged her back and looked up to find the other three kids running toward me.

"You're late." I heard Vincent's voice. He appeared in the doorway seconds later, cutting off the children running to me.

Funny, I didn't know the devil followed time.

I heard Emmett chuckle and realized I must've been thinking aloud by accident.

I considered apologizing but then decided against it. He already knew I didn't like him. Besides, he's never said sorry when he's offended me.

"Very classy, Rose. Dinner is ready and waiting on the table." He walked away and left us standing there.

Once he'd left the room, the rest of the kids ran to me, throwing their arms around me and talking a mile a minute.

"We got to get in there before he has a fit," Emmett interrupted.

We nodded, and Romeo led the way to the dining room.

Arriving at the table, I noticed Stephanie was already there, looking down at her plate. "Hey, Stephanie, how are you?" I asked once I was fully seated.

She looked up slightly, and it was then that I noticed her busted lip that she'd tried to cover up.

I zeroed in on it, and she jerked her head back down. "I'm doing very well, Rose. Emmett, how are you guys doing?"

I looked to Emmett, and he must have noticed too because his eyes darted to his father, and he had a look in his eye that I'd never seen him wear before. If looks could kill, I think Emmett would've murdered Vincent thirty different ways by now.

"Well, now that we've sat down, I figure we get right to it, considering we have already been delayed," Vincent said, looking from Emmett to me. "I wanted to talk to you about when I should be expecting grandchildren."

Two things happened at that exact moment. One, I choked and spat out my wine, and two, Emmett turned a very unhealthy shade of white—which, considering we were Italian, was bad.

"You two are not getting any younger, and you're going to need somebody to take over for you," Vincent continued.

I was grateful when Emmett chimed in because I was pretty sure I was frozen.

"I don't see how it's any of your business, Father, but when Rose and I decide to have children is between us. And we don't plan on it anytime soon, considering we haven't even been married a year yet."

I didn't know what Vincent had up his sleeve but let me tell you, whatever it was, I didn't like it one bit.

Looking over at Stephanie, I noticed a tear running down her face, but she wiped it away quickly.

Not wanting Vincent to notice, I shot out of my chair and pulled her chair out too.

"If you could just excuse us, I think I just got my period." I grabbed my purse and dragged her out of her chair, pulling her to the bathroom with me.

I closed the door once we got inside and pulled her into a hug. "Are you okay?"

I felt her sigh into my shoulder. "I'm okay, Rose, don't worry about me."

Pulling away, I grabbed my old cell phone out of my purse and placed it in her hands. "Here, I want you to keep this hidden. Emmett just bought me a new one so he can track me. He thinks I don't know about it, but I'm not dumb. My new number is already saved in it, and I want you to call me if shit ever hits the fan, okay?"

She put the phone on silent, shoved it underneath the sink, and looked up at me with a sad smile. "You are a really good person, Rose. I'm glad I have you."

I gave her a quick hug and opened the door. "Let's go before they start looking for us."

We said our goodbyes to everyone once dinner was over. Emmett and I were a little tipsy by the end of the night, so we had to call a driver and leave Emmett's car at Vincent's.

"Are we going back home or to a hotel?" I asked Emmett while we were walking to the car. It didn't take that long to get back to Chicago on the helicopter, but I wasn't in the mood to sit through an almost three-hour flight.

"I have a penthouse apartment here in New York we can stay at if you want."

"Yes, please. How long have you had this apartment?" I asked curiously.

"Well, it's actually my mom's. She must have bought it when I was young. I vaguely remember it." He shrugged.

We got into the car, and Emmett muttered an address to the driver.

It only took ten minutes to get to the apartment, and once we were inside, I was very impressed. I would never have wanted to live here and have a family here and all that, but the inside was quite beautiful.

It had a huge open floor plan with windows all around and a massive spiral staircase leading up to the second and third floor. It gave you the whole rustic feel without being too much.

While I looked out the window at the city, Emmett came up behind me. "Beautiful, isn't it?" he whispered into my ear.

I didn't know if it was the wine that was making this feel seductive or if I was just horny, but either way, I was going to pounce on him again if he kept it up.

"I'm going to go take a shower. Yell if you need anything."

He lowered his lips from my ear down to my neck and kissed me in that spot he knew used to make me weak.

I knew he was only doing this because he was drunk. Ever since we'd had sex, he'd made it a point to stay at least ten feet away from me.

I watched him walk away and contemplated my options. I could just go to bed and pretend that had never happened, or I could go in there and show him exactly what he was missing.

Of course, I chose the latter.

Emmett

As I got into the shower, I wondered if she would follow me. I would be lying if I said I didn't want to enjoy her body this time. I'd always told her she was the most beautiful woman I'd ever seen, and it was true.

I was already in the shower when I heard the door creak open. I jerked my head toward the sound and watched as she slowly took off her clothes, one article at a time, the little fucking minx.

She opened the door to the shower and walked in with a devious smile. "What did you think I was going to do? Go to bed?"

She dropped down onto her knees, gripping my dick in her delicate hands, and when she put her mouth on me, I had to tell myself not to come after only a few seconds like some inexperienced teenager.

It didn't help that the second she put my dick in her mouth, she took me all the way in, and I could feel my dick hitting the back of her throat. I'd taught her everything she knew, but the things she was doing with her tongue had me half thinking she'd lied about not sleeping with anyone else.

I was so close to coming in her beautiful mouth when she suddenly stopped and stood up.

"Let's go." She shut off the shower, and as I lifted her, she wrapped her legs around me, and I carried her out, kissing down her neck as we left the bathroom.

I gently laid her down on the bed with her legs still wrapped around me. As I ran my hands down her body, she tightened her legs and started pulling me closer so that I was right at her entrance, but I pulled back.

I wanted to take it slow this time. I knew I would be mad at myself in the morning for even doing this, but right now, I didn't give a fuck.

I ran my thumb over a nipple, only taking it into my mouth for a second before I let go, and she clawed at my back, silently begging me to give her my dick.

"Say please," I whispered just before I kissed the sensitive spot below her ear.

"No," she moaned, arching her back once I started kissing down her body.

I pulled my head away once I reached just above her pussy. "No?" I repeated. She let out a frustrated moan, and I chuckled. "I'm going to need to hear you say it, babe."

"Fine." She huffed. "Please."

In the same second that she said it, I slammed into her. I was glad we were alone in the penthouse because the moan she let out was so loud, I wouldn't have been surprised if the neighbors had heard.

My thrusts started slow, at an almost torturous pace. I gradually picked up my pace while she clawed my back some more. It was probably bleeding at this point, but I welcomed the pain.

I pulled out and flipped her over, lifting her ass into the air with a hard slap as I slammed back into her. I pounded into her even harder, then reached under to rub her clit while using my free hand to grab some of her hair, giving it a light tug, which sent her over the edge.

I felt her walls tightening as she came, and I spilled into her with short thrusts.

When we'd both come down from our high, I pulled out and walked into the bathroom to get a wet cloth so I could clean us off.

Returning to the room, she'd already flipped onto her back. I opened her legs and started to wipe away my cum. "I thought you had your period?" I laughed, and she shrugged a shoulder.

"I didn't want Vincent asking any questions."

I finished cleaning her and gave her ass one more slap before I walked back to the bathroom to get rid of the cloth, already feeling the guilt starting to creep in.

CHAPTER
Twenty

Rose

I WOKE UP ALONE AND WAS ANNOYED AT HOW DISAPPOINTED I was about it.

After we'd finished, he was so loving and gentle. He'd held me until we fell asleep and even kissed me goodnight. I had thought that after all that, things would be different.

Clearly, I was wrong, and this was just another Emmett mood swing.

Getting out of bed, I quietly dressed and grabbed all my belongings. Leaving the bedroom, I went in search of the living room. I got a little lost on the way, and even though this condo wasn't as big as our house, it was still a decent size, so it took me a little bit to find my way. I looked around when I finally reached the bottom of the staircase, and that was when I found Emmett on his phone at the table.

"Ready to go?" I asked from behind him.

"Yep," he responded without turning around.

"Did I do something wrong?" Ever since I'd reached my

breaking point at the wedding, I'd decided not to hold back when it came to my feelings. Once I crossed the bridge of destruction, there was no throwing that bitch in reverse.

"No, Rose. The helicopter's ready, and we have to get going," he replied flatly, not even bothering to look at me.

I tried to swallow my urge to cry. I'd finally let down some of my walls, ready to open up to him again, only for him to do this. It was as if I was eighteen all over again, and Emmett told me he didn't love me anymore. I put my head down in defeat and stared at the floor the whole elevator ride until we got to the roof and into the helicopter.

It was times like these that I wondered if I wasn't meant to have happiness. Maybe it just wasn't in the cards for me.

Once we arrived home, Emmett pulled up to the garage elevator and motioned for me to get out. I wanted to ask why he wasn't coming inside, but I decided against it and just kept going.

Walking into the house, Lorenzo was at the kitchen island, giving me a bright smile, but when I looked up at him, he instantly frowned when he saw my face. I didn't know if it was the comfort of seeing Lorenzo or the fact I was away from Emmett, but I instantly burst into tears.

Lorenzo quickly got up and wrapped me up in a hug. He reminded me so much of Sammy, which, in turn, made me cry even harder.

"Shh, it's okay, Rosie. I'm sorry," he said while stroking my hair. "Maybe we should visit your parents? Or maybe Claire? You haven't seen anyone in a while. Maybe it will brighten your mood and bring you a little distraction."

I pulled back and wiped my face on the back of my sleeves, giving Lorenzo a nod.

"Okay. I'm going to grab my keys while you go freshen up, and we'll get going," Lorenzo said before walking away.

We went to my parents first, which in turn just made my mood even worse. Mom didn't come out of her room, and Dad just smelled like alcohol.

Some things just never changed.

Pulling up to Claire's house, I knocked on the door, and thankfully, Tommy answered.

When he saw it was me, he gave me a big smile. "What's up? I haven't seen you in a while. How's married life treating you?"

I gave him a frown and looked down, shrugging my shoulders at him. His eyes went wide, and the next thing I knew, he was yelling Claire's name across the house.

"What the fuck are you yelling about, you fucking—" She stopped short when she saw me in the doorway and gave me a sad smile. She walked the rest of the distance to me and wrapped her arms around me, sighing. "Oh, Rosie."

I buried my face in her shoulder and allowed a few more tears to fall. "I don't understand what I'm doing wrong."

Claire walked us into one of the spare rooms nearby and sat me down on the couch before taking a seat beside me. She handed me a throw pillow and grabbed one of my hands.

"What happened?"

I told her the whole story, from the first time we fucked to this morning. When I finished, she grabbed both sides of my face and smiled at me.

"You are the strongest person I know, and before you roll your eyes, hear me out." She let out a breath and let go of my face. "You have gone through things that I wouldn't wish upon anyone, and yet you still managed to put a smile on your face and be the kindest person I've ever met. Even after Emmett broke your heart at such an awful point in your life, you were still willing to open up to him again. Don't you ever think that you're doing something wrong. Don't let his faults lead you to believe it has anything to do with you. He has battles he needs to fight on his own."

Her words did make me feel a little better, but it didn't change the fact that even though his faults were in our way, I didn't know how much more I could take before I reached my limit.

CHAPTER
Twenty-One

Rose

For Lorenzo's birthday, I'd decided to throw a big-ass party to show my appreciation.

He's always done a lot for me, and even though I knew it was his job to watch over me, I also knew that I was like family to him.

He was turning twenty-seven, which wasn't a significant milestone, but if I was being honest, I welcomed the distraction that planning a huge party would bring me.

I contemplated calling Claire and asking her to come with me to the decoration store because although she hadn't talked to me about it, I knew something was going on between her and Lorenzo and I didn't know if she would agree to come, so I settled for a text, asking what she was doing.

In true Claire fashion, she called right away. I swear she was allergic to text messages.

"Hello?" I answered.

"I can be there in five," she rushed out and hung up the phone.

Sometime later, I heard the doorbell ring. I was about to open the door when Lorenzo rushed in front of me, gun in hand, and flung open the door.

Claire scoffed and shoulder-checked him as she walked in.

"Sorry, Lorenzo, I forgot to tell you Claire was coming over." He gave me a tight nod and walked away.

"Where's the husband?" Claire turned to me and rolled her eyes.

"Who knows. I haven't seen him in weeks." I shrugged.

Two weeks and five days, to be exact. Ever since we got back from New York, and he dropped me off at home, he would be gone before I woke up and come home after I fell asleep. Anytime I went to the office to work, he was either in a meeting or "busy." On the nights I summoned enough courage to talk to him, I tried to wait up for him, but I swear he checked the security cameras just to make sure I was asleep before he'd come home.

She frowned and opened her mouth to say something, but I didn't really want to talk about it, so I forced a smile and shook my head.

"Let's just go to the store."

Today was Lorenzo's birthday, and I'd managed to convince Claire to help me out with setting up, reluctantly, but helping none the less.

I texted Emmett about the party, asking if he could keep Lorenzo out of the house for a few hours, but all I got back was a text saying, "Okay."

He didn't even ask if I needed any help. I mean, I would've said no, but still.

Claire and I had finished setting everything up, called in the extra security, and we were ready for the arrival of the guests.

In hopes that Emmett would make an appearance, I'd pulled out all the stops with my hair and outfit, curls down my back, and a hot as fuck black strappy dress that I knew would make him crazy. I touched up my lipstick and strapped on my heels just as Claire came out of the guest room, wearing a lace bralette and a high-waisted skirt.

I laughed and shook my head at her. "You are one evil woman, Claire Rosario. You're going to torture the man—and on his birthday, no less. Are you even capable of mercy?"

She winked, and we'd made our way downstairs when the doorbell rang.

After about twenty minutes, everyone had arrived. I texted Tommy and told him to take Lorenzo's guns before they came in, just in case we scared him, and he decided to spray bullets at everyone.

He texted back, telling me they'd just parked and were heading to the elevator.

"Okay, everyone," I yelled and told the DJ to stop the music. "He's coming up. Everyone, quiet." I rushed to turn off the lights and crouched down next to Claire.

The elevator opened, and just as they walked into the living room and turned on the lights, everyone jumped up and yelled, "*Surprise.*"

I was glad I'd told Tommy to take Lorenzo's guns because the first thing the man did was reach for it.

He was looking through the crowd and gave me a huge smile when he saw me. "You planned this?"

"Of course! I had to show appreciation to my brother from another mother." I smiled up at him.

He laughed and went to rustle my hair, but I quickly ducked and dodged his big-ass hands.

"Don't you dare," I said, reaching up and flicking him in the throat.

He laughed and pulled me in for a hug. "Thank you, Rosie. This means a lot to me. I honestly thought everyone forgot."

"Yeah, yeah, love you too, brat," I said, pulling away. "We doubled security, so you're off the clock. Now go get a drink and celebrate."

"Oh, no. You're coming with me, and so is Tommy and Claire. We're doing a birthday shot, so let's go." He pulled me toward the bar, and I then grabbed Claire. As I pulled Claire, she grabbed Tommy, and I was extremely proud that this human chain didn't knock anyone down. Ten points.

Lorenzo poured four shot glasses full of whiskey and handed them out. Claire refused, saying something about someone having to stay sober and making sure the party didn't get too wild.

Lorenzo shrugged, keeping her shot for himself, and lifted his shot in the air, yelling at the DJ to cut the music.

"I appreciate the fuck out of all you. Cheers, motherfuckers." Lorenzo yelled to the crowd.

"Cheers," everyone yelled, and we all threw our shots back.

Claire poured another round for us, and I threw it back quickly, sliding my shot glass back for her to pour me another.

After the third shot, I started feeling it, so I decided not to drink anymore. I got sad whenever I drank too much, and I didn't want to ruin Lorenzo's night, so I was going to stop while I was ahead.

I went to the dancefloor with Claire, and just when we started dancing, some guy came up behind Claire, whispering in her ear, probably asking her to dance. I was surprised when I saw her nod and start to grind on him.

I looked around for Lorenzo because although I was a little bitter about my current relationship, I didn't want to see him hurt.

I found him against a wall with one girl shaking her ass against his dick while he was making out with another, so I guess he was good. I swear I wanted to grab both of them by the throat and shake them.

Now that Claire had gone off and deserted me, I had to find a new dance partner.

I was surprised when I saw Tommy standing against the wall by himself. I'd never seen him without a girl wrapped around him.

"Come here, big guy, and dance with me," I yelled to him.

Tommy looked around, probably thinking I was talking to someone else.

I laughed and pointed at him. "I'm talking to you, Thomas."

He grinned and pushed off the wall, taking my hand. "Your husband's not going to try to kill me because of this, right?"

I let out an annoyed huff. "I doubt it. He's only in this because he has no choice."

Tommy and I danced for what felt like hours, and I had to admit it felt good to let loose and have fun.

Tommy and I used to be closer when we were younger. He was that guy friend every girl had who was always flirting unintentionally, but you didn't mind because it made you feel a little better about yourself. The fact that he was hot as fuck just added to the compliments he gave. It had always been platonic between us, but I wouldn't sit here and say that I hadn't had a fantasy or two—because I sure as hell had.

All in all, he was just really fun to be around, and I hated that I didn't see him much anymore. He only came to visit during important parties, holidays, and summer. He went to college three hours away, but I didn't blame him because his parents were real pieces of work.

The song changed to a slow one, and I was about to go tell the DJ no slow songs when Tommy pulled me back and put his arms around me. "I know you chose me to dance with to make him jealous," he said in my ear. I pulled back to deny it when he shook his head at me. "Don't worry about it. I'm using you too."

I frowned up at him, trying to understand what he meant by that, but he just pulled me closer and buried his nose in my hair. I let out a sigh and rested my head on his shoulders, swaying with him to the song.

Sometimes, I wondered what my life would have been like if I hadn't been with Emmett. Like, maybe I would've ended up with Tommy, or maybe somebody entirely different or maybe been alone, but then I remember that what-ifs were pointless.

Tommy and I had never been like that. We'd joked and flirted, but it was never anything deeper.

He was right, though. I was using him.

Emmett had always hated how flirty Tommy was, and I knew it was juvenile, but I was just so desperate for anything from Emmett, whether it be good or bad.

I just wanted some type of reaction to tell me that it wasn't only me, that he still had some type of feelings for me, and that I didn't see something that wasn't there.

I looked down in embarrassment, but Tommy put his finger under my chin, lifting it back up and cupped my cheek.

"Your fight's leaving you, Rosie. I can see it in your eyes. The universe hasn't been good to you, but you've taken every hit, and you're still going. It kills me to look at you now and see the spark leave your eyes. Your brother was so damn proud of you and your fight. It would break his heart if he could see how broken you are." I felt a tear slide down my face, but Tommy caught it for me before it fell. "Pick your head up, Bee. You can't see the stars down there."

I looked up at Tommy. I didn't know what to say for a while, but we stood there, looking at each other. It wasn't until now that I noticed his spark was gone too.

"You're right. We've lost our way, but we'll find it again someday—we have to." I reached up and kissed him on the cheek. "I'm going to bed. I'm exhausted."

With the party still in full swing, I went up to my room and slipped into bed, not even bothering to change.

It wasn't long before I fell into a deep slumber.

It was almost three in the morning when something woke me. I turned on my lamp and had to stop myself from screaming when I saw someone sitting in the corner of my room.

When my eyes finally adjusted, I saw that it was Emmett.

The room smelled of alcohol, and looking down, I saw he had an almost empty bottle in his hands.

"What the fuck, Emmett. You scared the shit out of me. You can't just sit in my room in the dark."

He took a long swig of the bottle and continued to stare at me. I then noticed his eyes were bloodshot, and I wondered if it was due to lack of sleep or if he was just that drunk. Judging by the bottle being nearly empty, I was going with the latter.

This was the second time I'd ever seen Emmett plastered. I had seen him drunk a few times, but never like this. He didn't usually allow himself to be in a situation where he was so intoxicated that he couldn't think straight. It was a rare sight to see

Emmett Rossi out of control, and right now, I'd definitely say he was out of control.

"Did you have fun tonight?" he slurred. "Better yet, did you fuck him?"

He was probably talking about Tommy. If he had really been looking, he would've seen that I went to bed alone, but since he clearly wanted to put on a show, I would humor him.

Sitting up, I let out a small, somber laugh. "Fuck who, Emmett? You? Tommy? You gotta be more specific here."

His eyes flared, and he clutched the bottle tighter. "You know damn well who I'm talking about, Rose."

"And what if I did? Fuck him, I mean. Maybe I did fuck Tommy, right here on this bed. What would it matter to you?" I shouldn't provoke him, but it wasn't fair for him to disappear for days and just show back up when he was mad.

He abruptly stood, throwing the chair back and smashing the bottle against the wall. "You're mine!" he yelled at me. "We are married, Rose, or do you not remember that?"

"As if I could forget," I yelled back at him. "I'm in this big-ass house alone every damn day while you're off doing God knows what. I haven't seen you in two weeks, Emmett, and we fucking work together. If it really means that much to you, no, I did not sleep with Tommy. I'm loyal even when you don't deserve it."

He let out a long breath and sat on the side of my bed.

"I saw the way you looked at him, and I went crazy. I miss the way you used to look at me. You would look at me as if I hung the moon, but now you barely even look at me to begin with. In your eyes, I'm just another person who left you." He gave me a humorless laugh.

"There comes a point where sorry isn't enough. No apology can even begin to repair what has been broken. I know that, but I lost everything, too, when Sammy died. And before you say it,

I know I'm the reason I lost you, but it doesn't make it hurt any less. I was dealt a really shitty hand, and I couldn't switch out the cards. I know I've hurt you. I will never forgive myself for the things I've done, and I'm not asking you to either, but I want to try to make this work. I'm sorry I've been MIA. After I got another taste of you in New York, I wanted more, but there are some things you need to know before we move forward, and I couldn't trust myself to keep my hands to myself, so I thought it would just be better if I stayed away until I could gather up the balls to tell you."

"Okay, what is it?" I reluctantly asked.

"Tomorrow. I need to be sober for this conversation." He grabbed my hand and kissed it. "Do you forgive me?"

"Not even close." I pulled my hand back. "You have to work for that."

"Fair enough," he said with a chuckle. "Can I sleep in here, though? Someone's in my bed, and I'd rather sleep next to my wife tonight."

"Fine, but stay on your side."

CHAPTER
Twenty-Two

Rose

OPENING MY EYES, I INSTANTLY FELT A POUNDING headache and the urge to throw up, which was annoying, considering I only had three shots, and the most I'd got out of it was a thirty-minute buzz.

A hand that wasn't mine moved up my stomach a little, and I let out a tiny squeal before everything came back to me, and I remembered my conversation with Emmett. I was shocked he was still in bed. I thought he would have woken up and left, going back to cold Emmett.

I lay in bed for a couple of minutes, just enjoying the feel of having him next to me. I didn't want him to think I'd already forgiven him for disappearing just yet, so I slowly slid out of his grasp, but the second I stood up, nausea hit me full force, and the next thing I knew, I was racing into the bathroom, barely making it to the toilet before I threw up.

After another two whole minutes of straight dry heaving, I felt a little better. I quickly brushed my teeth and went into the closet to grab some clothes. I peeked over at the bed, wondering if my throwing up had woken Emmett, but he was still dead asleep, snoring away.

I finished getting ready and was walking out of my room when I saw Lorenzo sneaking out of the guest room that I was positive I'd given Claire yesterday.

I wondered how that came about considering the last time I saw the both of them, one was shaking her ass for some random, and the other was dancing and making out with not one but two randoms at the same time.

After Lorenzo left, I slipped into the room, and I saw Claire under the covers, pretending to sleep.

I took a pillow from one of the chairs and threw it at her. "I know you're awake, you harlot. I saw him leave."

She threw the covers off her face and laughed. "Here I was thinking I was slick."

"Not trying to pry, but the last time I saw you both, you were preoccupied with different people, so how'd this happen?"

She let out a long sigh. "I don't know, Rosie. Sometimes he's so sweet, and other times he's just a whole other person."

"He's a Gemini, Claire, two faces and all that." I shrugged my shoulders. "Don't get me wrong, I'll never understand the inner workings of a Gemini, and I don't think anyone ever will, but you just gotta ride the wave."

"Yeah, well, I don't know how much longer I can stay in the water." She frowned, fidgeting with the seam of the blanket.

"Wow. That was deep. Let's go into the kitchen and eat our sorrows." I pulled the blankets off her.

She threw her hand in the air and pointed to the ceiling. "To the kitchen," she said, but as she went to jump off the bed, her foot got caught, and she smashed onto the floor.

I waited a few seconds to make sure she wasn't really hurt,

but when she gave me a thumbs-up, the laugh I'd been holding in burst out. I was holding my stomach, hunched over when she grabbed my ankle, and the next thing I knew, I was going down too.

"I guess I deserved that. I think I peed a little, though," I said as I wiped the tears from my eyes.

Claire finally got up and held her hand out to help me up. "What do you say we sneak out and eat breakfast somewhere else?"

"Yeah, definitely. Let's go."

CHAPTER
Twenty-Three

Rose

I'D BEEN REALLY DIZZY FOR THE PAST TWO DAYS, AND AFTER almost passing out this morning, Lorenzo decided to drag me to the doctor. He wanted me to call Emmett, but I insisted that we leave him be.

Emmett had been having some trouble with work and had to take a last-minute business trip the day after Lorenzo's birthday party. I was really disappointed when he told me because I had been hoping he was going to tell me whatever it was that he'd needed to get off his chest, but I guess it was going to have to wait.

Although I was pleasantly surprised because he'd been texting and calling daily to ask how I was doing.

Lorenzo and I were called in, and a nurse took my blood to run a few tests. She then ushered us into a room and told us the doctor would be in shortly.

"I can't believe you had to leave the room when they took my blood. You're a criminal, Lorenzo, aren't you used to it by now?"

When the nurse first pulled the needle out, his face went so pale that I thought he was going to pass out, and when she tied the rubber band around my arm, he'd bolted out of the room like his ass was on fire.

He looked at me, still looking horrified. "It's not the blood part as much as the 'needle going into you' part. I've never liked it."

"Okay, big guy," I said with a laugh.

He flipped me off at the same time the doctor walked into the room.

"Well, good afternoon," he said, eyeing the both of us in confusion. He extended his hand toward me to shake. "My name is Doctor Hammond. What seems to be the problem?"

"Well, I've been dizzy the past couple of days., I figure I'm fine, but this guy"—I pointed to Lorenzo—"thinks my days are numbered."

The doctor chuckled. "Well, I can assure you it's quite the opposite, actually."

When he didn't go into detail, Lorenzo and I gave him a questioning look. "What does that mean?" Lorenzo finally asked.

"Oh, right, sorry. Congratulations, you're pregnant!" He smiled at us.

Lorenzo looked like he was about to fall over, but I just laughed. "Very funny, but seriously, tell me what's wrong so I can go home and eat a sandwich."

"I can assure you, Mrs. Rossi, I'm not joking. You're a few weeks along. I don't have the proper equipment here to show you, but be sure enough, there is a baby in there." He turned to Lorenzo. "Are you the dad?"

Neither of us answered, too shocked to even speak, so the doctor just awkwardly cleared his throat. "Okay, well, I'll give you two some privacy to talk, and whenever you're ready, just go to the front desk, and they can give you a referral to a good OB-GYN. It was very nice meeting you, Mrs. Rossi."

He nodded at both of us before shutting the door.

Lorenzo went into full panic mode and started pacing the room. "He's going to kill us," he kept repeating.

I was so in shock that I didn't even bother to question what he was going on about.

He stopped pacing and looked up at me with wide eyes. "What are we going to tell him? Emmett's going to kill me. How did this even happen? When did this even happen? Who's the dad? Well, it doesn't even matter because he's going to kill him too. Please tell me it's not Tommy. I saw the two of you at my party. Oh, fuck, it's Tommy, isn't it? We're fucked." He kept rambling.

"Will you shut the hell up?" I said, hoping off the table. "It's Emmett's."

Leaving the room, I could practically feel the sigh of relief Lorenzo let out from behind me.

"Thank God," he said while following me out.

On our way home, I tried to wrap my brain around the fact I was having a baby. Emmett and I had been so back and forth. We were in no position to bring a child into the world. He was still hot and cold, and I felt like we'd just found a good middle ground where I didn't hate him. Would this set us back even further? Would he even be happy?

All this thinking was giving me a headache.

We drove up to the house, and even though it was still early, I decided to go to sleep and worry about my problems tomorrow.

CHAPTER
Twenty-Four

Rose

E MMETT TEXTED ME TO LET ME KNOW HE GOT BACK
early in the morning, only stopping at home for a minute
to change, before he had to hurry to the office, and that
he'd see me when I got there.

I was going to tell him about the baby when I got to work,
figuring the longer I waited, the harder it would be. But then I
changed my mind again, deciding I didn't really want to have this
conversation at work. I would just wait until we got home later.

We'd talked about having kids when we were younger, but
I couldn't help but wonder what his reaction would be. Part of
me thought he would be happy, but the other part was worried
he would be mad we were so careless. The last thing I wanted to
see in his eyes was regret.

I walked into the walk-in closet to get ready when my phone
started ringing. Thinking it was Emmett and that Lorenzo had accidentally let it slip, I rushed to pick it up, but my heart dropped
when I saw the caller ID.

Stephanie.

With shaky hands, I swiped to answer. "Hello?"

"Rose?" a squeaky little voice said. "It's Romeo."

"Yes, sweetie, what's wrong?" I tried to contain my nerves, not wanting to freak out and stress him out.

"Well, Mom said that if something's ever wrong to use this phone and call you, so I'm calling you because Gianna's really sick, and she needs her medicine, but I don't know where it is. Dad was yelling yesterday, and I haven't seen Mom since. I checked her room, but she's not there, and Dad left, and Gianna won't stop crying, and I need your help, please."

"Okay, Romeo, I'll be there as soon as I can. Keep this phone with you, and if your dad comes home, I want you to hide it, okay? Don't tell him you talked to me."

"Okay, thank you. Please hurry." Then he hung up.

I thought about calling Emmett to tell him what was going on, but I knew he had a lot of important meetings today, and I didn't want to bother him. But I also wasn't dumb enough to go to the devil's castle alone so I go with good ole reliable. Lorenzo.

"*Lorenzo,*" I yelled as I was leaving the closet.

He barged into the room with his gun drawn. "What's wrong? Are you okay?"

"Oh, I'm fine. I just need you to take a quick trip to New York with me." I added in a shrug, trying to make it sound like it was no big deal.

"What? A quick trip? What are you, crazy? For what?" He threw his hands in the air with each new question.

"I need to go check on Emmett's siblings. Gianna's sick." I tried to sound relaxed, not wanting him to see my panic and call Emmett.

"Can't they have someone a little closer to them figure it out?"

"No. They called me, so can we get to it? We can call the helicopter on the way and get it ready to go."

"Have you called and told Emmett?" he asked.

I contemplated telling him the truth, but I didn't have the energy to argue. "Yeah, he said okay, but I have to take you with me, so can we go now?"

He gave me a tired sigh. "Yeah, let's go."

I shot Emmett a quick text so that he didn't get worried when I didn't show up to the office.

Rose: Hey, my stomach's hurting. I'm going to stay home today. Good luck with all your meetings! I'll see you later.

My father had always taught Sammy and me to go with our gut. That if we felt like something was off, we needed to believe it and prepare ourselves. The worst thing that could happen was to be blindsided by something.

Walking up the stairs to Emmett's father's house, I got the feeling something was about to go down.

At first, when Romeo had called me, I knew something had happened, but I didn't think it was anything too bad. But the closer we got, the more I started to get the feeling.

I could just turn around and let it be, but I couldn't live with myself if something happened to the kids, and I was right there.

I looked to Lorenzo, and he must have felt it, too, because he pulled his gun out and handed it to me before pulling out another one from his ankle for himself and giving me a nod.

I opened the door, and it was silent.

Lorenzo went in before me, and we both looked around for the kids, but there was no one around.

I went up the stairs to Gianna's room and let out a very slow breath when I spotted the top of Natalia's ponytail poking out from the other side of the bed.

They all looked up as I got farther into the room, and I saw their eyes light up.

"I need you guys to stay up here, okay? I'm going to go find Romeo and your mom. Go into the bathroom and lock the door until I come back for you." They gave me a nod, and I walked back out.

Lorenzo met me outside the bedroom door. "There's no one on the first or second floor. I checked all the rooms."

"The three youngest are in here. I told them to wait in the bathroom, but that still leaves Stephanie and Romeo."

We were walking into the kitchen when I sighed in defeat. "Maybe Vincent came home and took them out of the house."

I turned to the left and saw a barely noticeable crack on the wall, and then it hit me. "The basement," I whispered, running up to the hidden door.

As I was about to open it, Lorenzo stopped me. "I'll go first."

He slowly opened the door, and I followed him down the stairs. I tightened the hold on the gun in my hand and mentally prepared myself to see some crazy shit, but when I reached the bottom step, never in a million years did I expect to see what I was seeing.

"Oh, my God." I covered my mouth with my free hand, freezing at what was in front of me.

"She's still breathing," Lorenzo said, pointing to Stephanie. "See? She's going to be fine, but we have to get her to a hospital."

I was still frozen, unable to move, my hand still over my mouth, and Lorenzo gave me a confused look. "Here, just help me get her." He started walking to her but stopped when he realized I wasn't following him.

Lorenzo walked back the few steps and nudged me. "Stephanie will be fine. She's breathing. That's a good sign. She's probably just passed out." He followed my line of sight when he realized it wasn't Stephanie that I was looking at and lifted his gun back up. "Who's that? Why are you crying?"

Lorenzo wouldn't know the woman whose ankle was currently chained to a wall a few feet from a very unconscious Stephanie because Lorenzo had never had a chance to meet her.

Hearing voices, she looked up, and her eyes widened. "Rosie?" She gasped.

"Who are you?" Lorenzo asked, still pointing his gun at her.

Unshed tears built in her eyes, and my heart broke for her a little bit, so much pain and fear in a single gaze.

"Is someone going to answer me?" Lorenzo said beside me. "What's going on? We've got to get out of here." He put a hand on my shoulder to get my attention. "Rose, who is she?"

I could tell he was getting frustrated, but I was just so shocked that I didn't even know what to say. I put my hand on his gun and lowered it.

"Emilia," I whispered to him.

Emilia's gaze landed behind me, and everything happened so fast. I heard someone scream at the same time a gun went off, and Lorenzo jerked back, almost dropping to the ground. He started to fire back but got hit again.

He looked at me and yelled something, but there was so much going on, and my head wasn't sending the signals to my legs to fucking move.

It wasn't until I saw Romeo on the ground, pulling on my foot, trying to get me to move, that I finally snapped out of it. I quickly looked around, scanning the room, and I saw six guys down on the floor.

I grabbed Romeo and led him to Emilia, handing him off

when I reached her. I quickly ran to Stephanie and dragged her behind the bed next to Emilia to take cover.

"Stay here. Don't move," I said to them, loud enough so they could hear me over the shooting.

I looked back up, trying to come up with a game plan, and I saw that there were still two more guys shooting in Lorenzo's direction, and a little farther back, sitting at a desk with his arms crossed and watching me with a smile was Vincent.

The other men weren't paying me any attention, so I lifted the gun and fired two shots at one of the guys, hitting his chest.

The other guy finally noticed me and started firing in my direction. I dropped down to avoid the bullets, and that was when I found a knife sitting on the floor beside me. Without giving it too much thought, I hurled it at him. I just needed a few seconds of distraction so I could go in for the kill. I got him right in the eye and finished him off with a bullet to the head.

I had to admit, apart from the beginning when I froze, I thought I'd handled that pretty well.

I heard a deep chuckle coming from behind me and groaned when I remembered Vincent was here. Turning, I pointed my gun at his head, causing him to laugh even more.

"It's so good to see you, Rose," Vincent said, moving to sit up straighter. "I must admit, I thought my guys were stronger than this, but if I had known you were a good shot, I would've brought more men," he said with another chuckle. "I see now that I've always underestimated you. I thought I had broken my wife well enough long ago, but you started coming around, and all of a sudden, she starts coming up with these ideas and plans, becoming quite bold if you ask me. Then I find out my son is calling you for help? Loyalty is a rare attribute in this house, I guess."

When I didn't respond, he leaned back again, holding both hands out. "Well? What are you waiting for? The way I see it,

Rose, you can either shoot now or wait until more of my men get here, which shouldn't be long." He looked down at his watch. "You're looking at about twelve minutes now."

"And what makes you think I'm scared of more men? I just started having fun. You clearly saw what I'm capable of." I walked up to the man with the knife in his eye, and I pulled it out, wiping the blood on his shirt. "Worry not, though, because as much as I'd love to prolong your death, I have things to do. I'll make this one as quick and painful as possible," I said with a sadistic smile.

"Well, if you do that, you won't be able to ask me any questions." He grinned at me. "Aren't you the least bit curious about what happened to your dear Samuel, or do you already know?"

I froze, and my heart stopped the minute I heard my brother's name coming out of this piece of shit's mouth.

He started to laugh. "That's definitely a no. I can see I've got your attention now, though. Ten minutes, Rose."

He looked past me, and his eyes lit up in pure joy. "Perfect," he continued, "the gang's all here. Why don't you ask him what happened to your dear twin? He's the one who pulled the trigger, after all."

I felt a hand on my shoulder, and I quickly turned around, ready to shoot, but when I looked up, I saw Emmett looking back at me with a pained expression on his face.

Turning back to Vincent, I gave him a withering look. "You're lying."

He was smiling at me again, and I could tell he was really enjoying this. "Oh, but I'm not. Why don't you ask him if you don't believe me?"

I turned to Emmett and looked up at him, shaking. "He's lying, right?" I searched his eyes, hoping that it wasn't true. He knew what Sammy meant had to me. He would never have betrayed me like that.

167

"Emmett, tell me he's lying. You would never do that to me."
He still didn't respond, but looking into his empty black eyes, I
knew Vincent was telling the truth. I was desperate for Emmett
to tell me he didn't kill him even if he really did because I didn't
know if I could come back from this. But the truth had a funny
way of always being right there, just waiting to come out, and by
the dead look in his eyes, I knew there was no doubt about it.

Emmett had killed my brother.

I was married to and having the baby of the man who had
killed my twin.

Betrayal could make the kindest person turn cold, and I
swear Vincent could see the transformation in my eyes because
his smirk dropped.

Did he really think I would spare him? That he was going
to get out of this?

I moved closer to him, then pointed the gun directly between his eyes and cocked my head to the side.

"Love is a weakness." And I pulled the trigger.

CHAPTER
Twenty-Five

Emmett

T HE LOOK ON ROSE'S FACE HAD ME TAKING A STEP BACK, wondering if I was next, but she quickly dropped the gun and ran to Lorenzo, who I just realized was on the floor, losing a lot of blood.

"We need to call someone," I said to Rose, but she ignored me and continued to put pressure on his wounds.

I quickly called one of the guys I knew who was a doctor close by and asked him to meet me at my penthouse.

I helped Rose carry Lorenzo to my car outside, and just as I was getting ready to hop in the driver's seat, she grabbed the keys out of my hand, not looking at me. "I'm taking him. There are things inside you need to take care of." She jumped in the car and sped off without another word.

Walking back into the basement, I stopped when I heard a woman's soft voice.

"It's okay, sweetie. Someone will be back soon, and then we can go."

The voice was so familiar that I paused for a moment.

I tried to place it, but I shook my head and continued my descent into the basement. I didn't have time to sit here and think. "Hello?" I called out.

Romeo popped his head out and ran to me, pointing behind the bed. "Emmett, you have to help. Mom's not waking up."

But instead of seeing Stephanie, my eyes caught someone else.

I didn't even realize I was walking until I was standing in front of a woman who looked almost identical to my mother. I rubbed my eyes, thinking my mind was playing a trick on me, but then she looked up at me and started to cry.

"Emmett?" she whispered. She got up, and that was when I noticed the chain around her ankle. "It's me." She gently put her hand on my face as more tears ran down her cheeks.

"Mom?" I questioned, thinking I was dreaming or something because there was no way I'd missed her the first time I was down here.

She nodded her head and pulled me into a hug. I hugged her back, breathing in her familiar scent, and I look down, following her chain.

It led to where my father was currently lying, and I snapped out of whatever state seeing my mom had put me in when I remembered more men were coming, and we needed to get the hell out of here.

I pulled away and grabbed both her arms. "We need to get out of here. I don't have any backup." I looked around for something to break the chain. Instead, I found a set of keys next to where Vincent had been sitting.

I quickly grabbed them, undoing her chain in record time.

"Go get all the kids. I'll grab Stephanie, and we'll meet out front. Hurry, Mom."

She gave me a nod, and we got to it.

Ten minutes later, we all got out of the car and went up the elevator into the penthouse.

All I could do was stare at my mom in disbelief. I kept blinking, wondering if she was going to disappear at any moment. I had no idea what to say. There were so many questions I wanted to ask her, but whenever I opened my mouth, nothing came out.

The elevator dinged open, and I rushed Stephanie in to get checked out by the doctor, and my mom followed quickly behind us with the kids hanging onto her. After putting Stephanie down, I ushered my mom and all the kids into one of the upstairs rooms and turned on some cartoons for them.

Going into the bathroom, I threw some water onto my face. So much had happened in the past couple of hours that I hadn't had any time to think.

I knew something was up when Rose sent me a text saying she was sick, and then a few minutes later, I got a text from some of my men, telling me the helicopter was all set and asking if my wife was ready to take off.

I immediately canceled all my meetings for the day and called a friend to hitch a ride to New York.

I tracked her phone to my father's house, and I panicked the whole way there, wondering why she would lie to me and go there alone. Then I started to think about what he could be doing to her. I'd never driven so fast in my life.

When I walked in, it was quiet at first, but then I heard guns go off, and I ran to the sounds, but it stopped the minute I found and opened the basement door. I thought my mind was playing tricks on me until I heard my father's voice.

I ran down the stairs and was finally able to breathe when I saw that Rose was the one with the advantage. That breath was short-lived, though, when I heard what he was saying about Sammy.

I watched as she pleaded with me to answer her, to tell her my father was lying. I could've lied, but then that would have kept me in the same place that I'd been in for three years. A coward who couldn't face the woman he'd betrayed in the worst way.

So, I remained silent, begging her with my eyes to forgive me. But looking into her eyes, I knew damn well that nothing in this world would change how she felt about me at that exact moment—pure hatred.

I saw the shift the moment she concluded that what my father was saying was true, and I swear the room dropped five degrees. She whispered something and then shot my father without so much as a blink.

The knock on the bathroom door stopped my thoughts from continuing. I quickly opened the door to find Rose on the other side.

"The doctor is finished with Lorenzo, so I'm taking him with me to my parents' house to recover for a while. I'll be staying there with him until I figure out my next move, and until then, I'm going to need you to do me a favor and leave me alone. Don't call me, don't text me, don't check up on me. Just don't do anything."

She walked away before I even had a chance to say anything.

I followed after her, but she turned around, giving me a cold dead stare, and pulled a gun out from the back of her pants. "Please don't make me do this. The least you can do right now is give me what I'm asking."

Nodding, I put my hands in my pockets and stepped back.

She lowered her gun and turned back around, continuing her exit.

I waited a few minutes, and with a sad sigh, I went back downstairs and sat next to my mom.

She pulled me into her embrace, and I laid my head on her shoulder.

"So, what happened?" I asked her, not moving.

She sighed and grabbed my hand. "While I was on my way to your school that day, somebody smashed into the side of my car, causing it to flip. The car rolled over a few times, and when it finally stopped, two men grabbed me and pulled me out. I thought they were helping me out until I was thrown into a car and knocked out. When I came to, I was in the basement. I looked up to see your father standing over me. He threatened to torture then kill you if I ever escaped. I tried to kill him a few times throughout the years, but the asshole was always two steps ahead of me."

She continued to tell me how she and Stephanie got to be very close and how she helped Stephanie raise my half-siblings.

Sometimes, Stephanie would sneak her some pictures of me and gave my mom updates on how I was doing. They'd made a plan to escape, but Vincent found some money that was stashed and beat Stephanie half to death.

"I heard what your father said to Rose before she shot him. I don't know what happened, but I do know you loved those two growing up, and you would never hurt either of them unless you had no choice. She'll come around. She just needs time, is all."

Maybe the Rose I knew back then would forgive me, but I wasn't so sure about this Rose.

CHAPTER
Twenty-Six

Rose

WE CAME TO A STOP OUTSIDE MY PARENTS' HOUSE, and I quickly got out, rushing around to open Lorenzo's door to help him out.

He put an arm around my shoulder, and we slowly made our way to the door, stopping right before we got inside. "For what it's worth, I know he loves you. Everything he does is in your best interest. I know you probably want space, and I'm on your side, always, but I do think that at some point, you should at least hear him out."

"Maybe one day," I said with a small smile. "Let's get you inside before you start bleeding again."

Lorenzo was in a lot of pain, so I didn't want to argue with him. I knew I couldn't avoid Emmett forever, but as of right now, it was still so fresh that the last thing I wanted to do was have a conversation with him.

I just couldn't wrap my head around the fact that not only was he there for Sammy's death, but he pulled the trigger. I always had a feeling Vincent was somehow involved in the murder, but damn, I sure as hell wasn't expecting Emmett's part in it also.

I hadn't seen my parents in a few weeks, and even though they were a mess these days, I would rather be here with them. The thought of being home with Emmett right now made my stomach turn.

My father saw us in the entry and ran up to help me with Lorenzo.

He didn't even ask me what happened. He just grabbed Lorenzo's other side and gave me a sad smile. Somebody probably already informed him I was coming.

"I'm sure you've already heard about most of what happened, but can it wait until tomorrow to go into detail? I'm exhausted, and I don't think I have enough energy to rehash the whole story."

He nodded. "Sure, no problem. I have a few meetings to discuss Vincent's death, but we can talk whenever you're ready."

Two of my father's men came up to grab Lorenzo from us, guiding him upstairs.

"Can we put Lorenzo in one of the rooms next to mine? I want to be close to him in case he needs me," I told the guys, and they both nodded, continuing up the stairs.

I grabbed our stuff and dropped it off in my room—well, my old room now—and I went in search of my mom.

Her bedroom door was open when I walked by, so I knew she wasn't in there. Doing a quick walk-through of the house, I found her in the library, smiling down at one of the old photo albums.

I stood in the doorway and watched her for a little while. It had been so long since I'd seen a smile on her face. It wasn't like the smile she used to wear but a smile no less.

She looked up at the sound of my footsteps as I entered the

room, and her smile dropped when she saw my current state. She quickly put the album down and opened her arms. "Come here, baby."

I picked up my pace and crawled into her lap once I reached her, laying my head on her shoulder.

"This life is a hard one to live by," Mom said as she kissed my head, "but I wouldn't trade it if it meant I couldn't have you and your brother. In a world full of death and darkness, I can still say I found my light. It's going to get hard before it gets easy, but you can't give up yet."

Mom pulled a tissue out of the box on the table and handed it to me. I quickly cleaned up my face, and she wrapped her arms around me.

A new wave of tears started flowing when she began to sing the lullaby she used to sing to Sammy and me before bed. By the end of the song, I felt my eyelids getting heavy, and it wasn't long before I was asleep.

I grabbed a tray of food from the kitchen to bring to Lorenzo and found him in bed, struggling to sit up. I frowned and instantly felt guilty for allowing myself to fall asleep without checking on him first.

"Need some help?" I asked from the doorway.

He looked up at me and huffed. "Have they gotten you a new bodyguard yet? I can't protect you in this state, Rosie. What if there's retaliation for you killing Vincent?"

"Trust me. I don't think anyone in the world will be mad that I offed him. If anything, they'll thank me. Besides, I'm going to be right here with you twenty-four seven. We can protect each other."

He went to reach for the water on the nightstand and winced.

I rushed over to him and gave him my arm so he could pull himself up easier.

Once he was finally in a sitting position, I handed him his water and then placed the food tray on his lap.

I felt terrible for Lorenzo. He had always been the protector, and now that he could barely move, he looked miserable.

After seeing him get shot, I thought I was going to lose him. He was lucky enough to only get hit in the shoulder and thigh, so it wasn't deadly, but the last thing I wanted to happen was for him to overexert himself and rip a stitch open, causing him to bleed out or something.

"I'm going to go change, and I'll come back after to see if you need anything, okay?"

"You don't need to worry about me, Rose. I'll be fine."

"Oh, shut up, would you? Let someone else take care of you for once." If he weren't injured, I'd punch him for being so stubborn.

He chuckled and waved me out. "Bye, Rose."

When I got into my room, I stripped off all my clothes and noticed there was blood on some of them so instead of putting them in the washer, I put them straight in the trash.

I took a quick shower, and once finished, I examined my belly in the mirror.

It was crazy to think that I would have a baby to care for in a few months, and even though it wasn't an ideal time, I was kind of excited.

I was rubbing my belly, looking for differences, when my door burst open, and Claire walked in, frantic.

I quickly moved my hands, but I mustn't have been fast enough because her mouth opened and closed, then opened again and closed again.

"What were you doing?" she finally asked.

I contemplated lying, but then again, she was going to find out eventually, so what was the point?

"I'm pregnant," I blurted out before I lost my courage to tell her.

"Oh, shit," she said, sitting on my bed. "Who's the dad?"

Seriously? "Who do you think? I have literally never slept with anyone else. Do you really think I'm going to start now? When I'm married?"

"You have a point. So when's your due date?"

"I have no idea. I have an appointment in two weeks to find out."

"Are you happy?"

"Honestly? I really am. I was surprised at first, but the more I thought about it, the happier I got."

"Are you scared?"

"No," I responded confidently.

I wasn't. I knew I was still young and that everything had gone to shit, but I would do right by my baby. I wouldn't allow the past to get in the way of me being a damn good mother.

When she didn't say anything else, I looked up to see that she was crying.

"Hey," I said with a frown.

She looked up at me, frantically wiping the tears.

"It's going to be okay," I reassured her.

"I'm happy that you're happy, and I'm glad you're not scared, but I'm fucking terrified," she replied, looking up.

I was about to go on a tangent about how everything would

be okay, but the distant look in her eyes stopped me. "You're not talking about me, are you?"

With fresh tears building in her eyes, she slowly shook her head. "I've known for three months already, and I don't know what to do. I'm not as confident about this as you are. My mom's going to disown me, and I don't know if I can do this by myself."

Taking a seat beside her on the bed, I took her hand in mine.

"And before you ask," she continued, "my baby's dad will not be in her life."

"It doesn't matter." I lifted her face to look at me. "It doesn't matter because you're one of the best people I know. And that baby? She's going to love you no matter what, and that's all you need." Wrapping her in a hug, I let out a heavy sigh. "It's okay to be scared, but you are definitely not alone. No matter what, you'll always have me right beside you."

CHAPTER
Twenty-Seven

Rose

I'D BEEN BUSY FOR A WHILE HELPING LORENZO OUT WITH everything, but now he was basically back to normal. I didn't plan on going back to work anytime soon, so for the past couple of days, I'd had a lot of time on my hands, time that I'd spent overthinking everything that had happened following that dreadful day.

I'd asked Lorenzo how everyone was doing a few times, but he was usually very vague about his answers, and I didn't want it to seem like I cared too much, even though a part of me wanted to grab his head and shake it for some more information.

At least today, I had my first obstetrician appointment to keep my mind off things. In the two weeks since I'd found out, my belly had grown super-fast.

I still hadn't told my parents about me being pregnant. I couldn't stand the looks of pity they gave me every time I walked into the room, so I could only imagine the kind of looks I would get if I told them that not only had I left my husband, but I was pregnant too.

"You almost ready?" Lorenzo peeked his head into my doorway.

"Yeah." I made my way out of the room and gave Lorenzo a quick hug. "Thank you for taking me and for not telling anyone. I really appreciate it."

"No problem, Rose." He smiled at me and nodded his head down the stairs. "Let's go before you're late."

"I don't like this place," Lorenzo declared as we took a seat, and I started filling out paperwork.

"What are you saying? We just got here, and it's one of the top-rated doctors' offices in the area. What don't you like about it?"

"Well, for starters, there's not even a thing to drink water from. What am I supposed to do if I get thirsty?"

"You are a different breed, Lorenzo Moretti," I answered with an eye roll.

"Rose Rossi," a nurse called from the hallway.

We got up to follow the nurse, but when she saw Lorenzo get up with me, she gave him a stern glare.

I looked from the nurse to Lorenzo and raised a brow at him in question, but he just shrugged at me.

On the way to the room, we saw what looked like a break room with a water cooler inside and a bunch of nurses standing around it.

"So that's where the water is." Lorenzo tsk-tsked. "All those people out there, and here they are, harboring the water for themselves." All the nurses looked over, and Lorenzo shook his head. "Disappointed," he yelled to them.

I burst out laughing, and the nurse leading us to the room turned around and gave Lorenzo another dirty look.

"Right in here, please," she said with a hint of annoyance.

Five bucks said he slept with her or maybe one of her friends, and she thought I was his pregnant wife who he'd cheated on.

"The doctor will be right in," she said as she walked out.

I put my stuff down, and Lorenzo turned around so I could take off my pants and get under the sheet.

"You might want to sit as close to my head as possible—unless you want a sneak peek at my goods." I laughed when his face turned red.

"Yes. Of course, sorry," he stammered, pushing his chair back.

A knock on the door made me jump, and seconds later, a man poked his head in.

"Hello, Rose, I'm Doctor Johnson." He smiled at me and shook my hand.

Hot damn, he was one beautiful man. Tall and muscled, with golden skin and dimples. Fucking dimples.

I was expecting someone older, but he had to be at the most in his early thirties. I half didn't mind the fact that he would be the one all up in my business.

The doctor turned to Lorenzo and stuck out his hand. "You must be Dad?"

I shook my head, and Lorenzo made a gagging sound beside me.

"Oh, my apologies. Well, first things first, I'm going to ask a few questions, and then we can do an ultrasound to see if we can find that baby of yours."

After what felt like eighty questions, a nurse rolled in a cart with a screen and a bunch of wires.

I pulled up my shirt and pushed the sheet down a little, and the doctor squeezed the gel onto my belly. I turned to Lorenzo and saw him watching the doctor's every move.

Lorenzo had never trusted others, but now that I was pregnant and I'd killed one of the higher-ups in New York, he was extra paranoid.

The doctor moved the wand around a few times and let out a soft "Huh."

We were all looking at the screen, but he hadn't pointed anything out, so I had no idea what I was looking at.

"Why did you just 'huh,'" Lorenzo barked at him.

"Well, it looks as though you're having twins!"

The last thing I heard was "Shit" from Lorenzo before everything turned black.

On our way back from the doctor's office to my parents' house, I could feel Lorenzo's gaze constantly searching my face to make sure I was okay.

After I'd come to, the doctor ran some tests and concluded that stress mixed with the lack of water had made me pass out. He also told me I was due around the beginning of November.

I'd made another appointment for a month from now to find out the gender of the twins.

Twins. I was having twins.

The doctor had managed to get a few pictures, and he handed them to us on the way out.

I guess now was as a good time as any to break the news to my parents. I felt like if I didn't talk about it, I was going to explode.

Lorenzo walked in before me and stopped short, causing me to crash into him and the pictures to fall onto the floor.

"Warn me next time, would ya? Precious cargo." I peeked around him to see what had made him stop so abruptly, and I sucked in a breath when I saw that it was Emmett.

He wasn't looking at Lorenzo or me, though. Nope, he was looking right at the sonogram pictures that had fallen on the floor. He must have been here for a meeting because my father came walking out of his office but stopped when he saw me.

"Rose, I didn't know you'd be back so soon." His words trailed off, and he followed Emmett's line of sight. My father was confused at first. I could tell he was trying to figure out what exactly he was looking at, but I saw the exact moment when the realization hit because his eyes nearly popped out of their sockets.

Emmett snapped out of his stoic state, and his eyes shot in my direction, first looking at my belly then up to my eyes.

"What's that?" he finally asked.

"Don't play dumb, Emmett. I think you know exactly what *that* is."

"How long have you known?" He had this crazed look on his face, staring at me dead in the eyes, and he hadn't even blinked.

"A few weeks now. The day before I found out you killed my brother, actually." I think every person in the room, apart from myself, flinched from the cold, harsh tone of my voice.

Emmett went to open his mouth, but it was my father who cut in.

"Sweetheart, I think it's time I tell you what happened. Can everyone come into my office?" He held his hand out to his office, and Lorenzo started toward it but stopped when he saw that I wasn't following.

He knew.

My father knew what happened, and he still had me marry him.

I gave Emmett and my father a withering glare. "The time for talking has come and gone. This conversation should have happened years ago."

"I think it's imperative that you know, Rose." My father exhaled loudly. "I promised Sammy I wouldn't tell you unless I had to, and I think the time is now."

He knew the mention of Sammy would change my mind.

"Fine." I huffed at him. "I just have one question before I move forward. Who's taking Vincent's place? I'll be damned if I allow my children to be brought up in such a disgusting environment."

"I don't know yet," Emmett chimed in, "but it's not going to be me."

With a huff, I picked the pictures up off the floor and walked into the office.

Everyone took a seat, and for a few minutes, no one said anything. Finally, my father took a deep breath.

"I took Sammy with me to New York to finish up a deal. It was supposed to be easy, shake a few hands and exchange a few things, but it was a setup. A few weeks before the meeting, Vincent was in Chicago and had made a comment about how he didn't mind you and Emmett dating because he loved seeing a young thing prancing around. Sammy didn't like what he was insinuating and pulled a gun on him, threatening to shoot him in the dick if he ever heard something like that come out of his mouth again."

He took another breath and continued. "Well, when we got to New York, we weren't there long before we were ambushed. I hadn't brought many men with me because it was supposed to be a clean-cut deal, so I was blindsided. Vincent tortured us for hours, Sammy getting the worst of it, and we thought we were going to die there—until Emmett showed up."

CHAPTER
Twenty-Eight

Emmett

Nineteen Years Old

I HATED LEAVING ROSE. THE SAD LOOKS AND PUPPY DOG eyes always made me weak.

She begged me to stay home because it was her birthday, and it was bad enough that Sam and her father weren't there to celebrate with her. But my father had demanded I go to him or he was coming here, and I didn't want him anywhere near Rose, so I had to go.

Hopefully, I could just go there, see what he wanted, and leave.

I opened the door to the warehouse and looked up to see my best friend and his father tied to a chair with blood running down their faces. Sammy was unconscious, and Mr. Romano looked like he was almost there.

"We've been waiting for you." My father came out of the shadows and poured water on Sam. "Now we can have some fun."

Sam woke up and looked around, probably trying to remember where he was.

"Now that everyone's here and awake"—my father picked up a gun from the table beside him and threw it to me, then pointed to Sammy—"kill him."

"What the fuck? No." I narrowed my eyes at him.

"See now, that's what I thought you'd say." He started laughing and pulled out a phone. "Don't worry, though. I'll get what I want."

He smiled and faced his phone toward us. "Now shoot him, or I'll have my men that are following sweet little Rose shoot her instead. Regardless, one of the Romano twins is dying today."

I pointed the gun at my father, and he laughed even harder.

"I thought you'd try this, too, but if my men don't hear from me in the next"—he looked down at his watch—"ten minutes, not only will they kill her but rape her first."

"Why are you doing this? What the fuck is wrong with you?" He was sick. Mentally ill or something. He had to be.

"Well, you see, Emmett, respect goes a long way. And Samuel here needs to learn that there are consequences to actions. Now, him or Rose. You pick, but just know that time's ticking."

He faced the phone to us again, and I saw a video of Rose and her friend sitting at one of Rose's favorite coffee shops. It took every ounce of power in me to not put a few bullets in my father's head.

I looked to Mr. Romano, hoping for a signal or something, anything to show me there was a way out of this, but he wouldn't even look up. I knew he was conscious because I saw him tense a few times.

I looked back at Sam and shook my head. "No, I can't do that."

"If he touches my sister, I'll kill you and him myself," Sam growled at me, trying to jerk his arms out of their hold.

"Six minutes," I heard my father whisper.

"Just do it, Emmett," Sam yelled, turning to his dad. "Don't tell Rose unless you have to. I know she'll feel guilty, but it has to be me."

"Five minutes," my father said.

Mr. Romano finally picked his head up and gave me a look of defeat. "It's okay, Emmett, just do it."

"Three minutes."

I wished everyone would just shut up so I could fucking think for a minute. There had to be a way out of this. A plan or something, I just needed a little more time. If only everyone would just shut the fuck up.

"Emmett," Sam yelled at me. "Fucking do it."

"Two minutes."

"Emmett," Sam yelled at me again.

I turned back to Sam and nodded my head at him. "I'm so sorry."

"Take care of her," he told me before turning to Vincent with a smirk. "I'll be waiting for you in hell, Vincent."

I numbed myself and pulled the trigger.

The shot that rang out echoed through the warehouse.

I heard my father's voice talking to someone. "Everything's all set. You can clear out."

He grabbed my shoulders, and I jerked out of his grasp. "Don't fucking touch me," I spewed at him. "I will never fucking forgive you for this, you sick piece of shit."

"Oh, but you will," he responded. "You don't have much of a choice now."

I untied Sammy, threw his body over my shoulder, and slipped a knife into John's hand so he could get himself out.

I was just about to walk out when John spoke up. "Prepare yourself for the war you've just caused, Vincent. It won't end well for you."

He shot up, throwing the knife at my father and hitting him in the shoulder. Grabbing the gun from my hand, he fired three shots at the men surrounding us, and they all started spraying bullets at John. He got hit in the arm, and I was pretty sure another hit his leg, but he continued to fire.

I ducked down with Sam's body still hanging over my shoulder, and I tried to pull John out of there before more guys came in, but he stood his ground.

"We have to leave. Now." I pulled him again, harder this time, but he jerked out of my grasp and got shot once more in the shoulder just as he ran out of ammo, but he still wasn't walking away. It was almost as if he wanted this. He wanted them to kill him.

"Please, Mr. Romano, they can't lose both of you," I pleaded with him.

John turned to me with wild eyes, and after what felt like forever, he finally nodded and let me lead him out.

CHAPTER
Twenty-Nine

Rose

MY FATHER FINISHED TELLING ME THE STORY, BUT I was more confused now than I was before.

"So how did you go from being at war to me marrying him?" I asked.

"New York and Chicago were at war for almost two years until finally, I couldn't take it anymore. There were so many lives lost that the guilt started to overpower me. I know this is what my men sign up for, but it was my fault that we went into New York unarmed. I couldn't let any more people suffer for my mistakes. I attended countless funerals and watched as family after family was ripped apart right in front of my eyes. And all because I wanted to avenge a son who was never coming back. So finally, the capo and I came to a truce, deciding you and Emmett would marry as a symbol of peace. I knew you two had been together before Sammy's death, and I also knew how in love you two were, so I figured it'd be okay."

"That's why you left me, isn't it?" I turned to Emmett. "Guilt.

You felt guilty for what you did, and instead of telling me the truth, you just left me to pick up the pieces on my own. Kicking me while I was down."

"What would you have done if I'd told you? You think it was easy for me to just leave?" Emmett was about to keep going, but I was done listening for today. There was too much coming at me, and I needed to think.

"Well, I guess we will never know what I would've done." I turned to my father. "Thank you for telling me, but I still need time to process." I grabbed Lorenzo's hand and pulled him to the door. "Let's go, Lorenzo."

We pulled up to the cemetery, and it kind of scared me how well Lorenzo knew me.

He knew exactly where I needed to be without having to ask.

He parked the car and turned it off, not moving to get out. "Did I ever tell you about my sister?"

He was trying to distract me, and I gladly welcomed it.

"You have a sister? I can't believe you never told me about her. Older or younger? Where is she?" I was actually kind of hurt that I never knew he had a sister. I'd known Lorenzo for years, and not once had he ever mentioned her.

"She was younger. Same age as you, actually."

I had a smile on my face for half a second before it dropped. "Was?"

Lorenzo looked at me and shrugged. "She died before I started working for your dad. I don't know if I've ever told you, but my dad was always in and out, and my mom did a lot of drugs. At that point, I was twenty, and even though I was so sick of my mom's bullshit, I stuck around for my sister. I had a plan, you know?" He looked back down and let out a huff. "I was going to wait until she'd graduated high school, then I was going to take her, and we were going to get our own place without our mom. Mom had made her bed, and I didn't want Delilah to suffer alone, with my mom always high looking for another hit.

"One day, I was out, and my mom came looking for me, said she owed someone money and that if she didn't give it to them soon, they were going to come after us. I thought she was just lying to try to get money out of me for more drugs, so I told her off. But when I got home later that night, I found Delilah in her room, lying in a pool of her own blood. She was shot four times. Twice in the chest and twice in her head."

He looked back up at me and grabbed my hand. "I guess what I'm trying to say is, I know what you're going through, but no matter what you do, it will never change the outcome. You're going to have a baby, two of them, actually. I know you're mad at him, but this is what Sammy wanted. Not a day goes by that I don't wish I had that option. I would give my life for hers in a heartbeat. He gave away his life so you could have yours."

Wiping my tears on the back of my sleeve, I reached over the center console and hugged Lorenzo.

Pulling back, I smiled sadly at him. "I'm so sorry about your sister, Lorenzo."

We got out of the car, and he walked me to Sammy's grave.

"I'll just be right over there." He pointed to a headstone a few spaces down. "I'm going to go say hi to Delilah."

"She's buried here?"

"Yeah." He smiled at me. "Today's actually her birthday."

CHAPTER
Thirty

Rose

I T HAD BEEN A LITTLE OVER A MONTH SINCE THE INCIDENT—
that was what I called it now—and I was going crazy.

My father and Lorenzo were scared New York was going
to retaliate and come after me, so I'd been locked away at my
parents' house, and I couldn't take it anymore. After thinking,
then thinking some more, I decided it was time to go back home.

Since I got here, I'd seen little pieces of my mom's old self
resurfacing, and that made me really happy, but the house was
still filled with too much sadness to make me want to stay.

The mood just felt so heavy, and every time I left my room,
I walked by Sammy's, and it was like a jab to the heart.

I hadn't noticed until Lorenzo said something to me the
other day, but during the past couple of months that I'd been
at Emmett's, I went from visiting Sammy twice a week to twice
a month. Going out and actually doing things had been good
for me and helped lift the dark cloud that had been above me

for years, but since I'd been back at my parents, I felt the cloud starting to return.

My parents didn't even argue about me leaving. They understood my need to be away, and I hoped one day they could leave too and find their happiness again.

"Ready to go?" Lorenzo said, grabbing my bags.

"Yeah." I smiled at him. I gave my parents a quick goodbye, promising to visit more often, and then we were out the door.

Last I heard, Emilia, Stephanie, and the kids were staying at Emmett's house. Well, technically, Emilia's now, I guess, since she was still alive, but either way, at least with them there, I would have people around to keep me company. Lorenzo told me that Emmett had been staying at his childhood home so he could be closer to me just in case I needed something.

Since the last time I saw him, he had texted and called me every day, asking how I was doing, how I was feeling, and if I needed anything. I never responded, so he always turned to Lorenzo and blew up his phone instead. And every day, Lorenzo told him I was fine and that I didn't need anything.

I knew this wasn't the end for us, especially now that we were going to have kids, but I still needed some time to process a few things and maybe ask a few more questions before I could move forward.

Lorenzo and I drove into the garage, and I was surprised at how relaxed I was at being back here after so long. I thought the anxiety would hinder me from even being able to step inside, but I actually felt fine.

I wondered if Emmett had told any of his family that I was pregnant. The bump was visible now, so if they didn't know, they were about to find out.

I had no idea how Claire managed to hide it for so long, considering she was a week shy of being in her third trimester.

I mean, I knew it was different when you only had one in there, but still, she was two months ahead of me.

I also wondered if Lorenzo knew she was pregnant. I knew they only had a fling, but I felt like it was going to be a little awkward. He had to know at this point, considering I'd accompanied Claire to every one of her doctor's appointments since I'd found out, and Lorenzo had followed. If he hadn't connected the dots by now, then he never would on his own.

We parked, and I noticed there was a bunch of new security everywhere. Considering Lorenzo and I hadn't been back in a while, I didn't know how this was going to go.

Dom and Damon were still the security outside, so we had no problem getting in through the gates, but I didn't recognize the ones at the elevator that led up to the house, and by the looks they were giving us, I had a feeling they didn't know who we were either.

One of the men walked up to my window while the other went to Lorenzo's.

"Name," the one at Lorenzo's door asked.

"Lorenzo Moretti and this is Emmett's wife, Rose."

"ID," the one at my window asked, tapping on the window that I hadn't fully opened just in case they tried something. You couldn't trust those you didn't know.

Lorenzo showed the guy on his side his ID, but I looked out the window and shrugged. "I don't have it on me. It might be in the trunk with my stuff, but I didn't know there would be a problem with me getting into my own house."

The guy at my window, who I'd officially named asshole, laughed. "I suggest you guys turn around and leave."

Was he joking?

I looked at Lorenzo, half wondering if this guy was serious.

When we didn't make a move to leave, the asshole pulled his gun out and pointed it at me. "Did I stutter? Leave."

Seriously?

I knew they were doing their job, but he didn't need to be douchey, and he definitely didn't need to pull a gun on me.

I looked over at Lorenzo just in time for him to see the gun, and I saw the rage flare in his eyes. He moved his hand to his pants, probably to get his own gun, but I quickly grabbed his hand, stopping him.

"I've got this," I said to Lorenzo with a smirk.

Lorenzo shook his head at me, pulling out not one but two pistols and pointing them at each of the guards at our windows. "You have five seconds to put that back, or this is not going to end well for you," he growled at the asshole.

I had been blaming the hormones, but I hadn't been able to release some anger in a very long time, so it looked like he was the lucky winner of my wrath.

I opened my window all the way, bent his wrist back so that his grip loosened on the gun, and I pulled it out of his grasp, turning it on him in one quick maneuver. It was so quick that even I was surprised.

I grabbed him by the ear and pulled him closer to me. With my finger on the trigger and the safety off, I pointed it at his left eye.

"Listen here, asshole, and you listen good. What I would like to do is go inside and see my mother-in-law. I've been in an awful mood, so I just want someone to fawn all over me for a little while and hopefully make me some food considering I'm eating for three, but I can't do that because you want to see a fucking ID. Well, let me tell you something, you don't have to worry about is what my husband's going to do when he finds out how you've treated me because I'm about two seconds away from taking this gun, shoving it up your ass, and emptying the clip. Not to mention—"

The sound of a door slamming and footsteps cut me off.

"What's going on?" I heard Lucas before I saw him, and I let out a little laugh because he must've seen me in the security feed.

I let go of asshole's ear and opened my door, slamming the asshole with it in the process, causing him to fall to the floor, and I jumped out of the car, hugging Lucas. "I've missed you." I really had. I'd spent a lot of time with them when I was here, and it had sucked being away from them.

Lucas pulled back and smiled at me. "I've missed you too, my little assassin. I've had to eat takeout every day, and it's no fun." He looked at the security guards and gave them a glare. "This is Mr. Rossi's wife, Rose."

"Come on, Lorenzo." I gave the asshole a dirty look and put the gun's safety back on before throwing it to his partner.

When I walked inside, it was quiet at first. I almost thought nobody was home until I walked into the living room and saw everyone sitting on the couches, watching a movie.

"Hey, guys," I said with a smile.

Everyone turned to me simultaneously, and the next thing I knew, I was being pulled into a group hug. Emilia and Stephanie were on both sides of me, and they each kissed me on the cheek.

Everyone pulled back except for Stephanie and Gianna.

"I never got to thank you for everything." Tears started to form in Stephanie's eyes. "I can never thank you enough for all that you've done for me."

She pulled me in for another hug, and I wrapped my arms around her.

"Don't worry about it. You can always count on me."

Stephanie pulled away, and I was left with the kids and Emilia.

Emilia stared at me for a little bit with a bright smile on her face. "Rose Romano." She walked up to me and palmed my face. "I always knew you'd be beautiful when you grew up. My son is one lucky man."

I frowned at her mention of Emmett, and she gently placed her hand on my belly and smiled.

"Come take a walk with me." She locked her arm with mine and pulled me down one of the hallways. She opened the last door on the right of the hall, right across from Emmett's room, and I was stunned when I looked around and saw that it was a beautiful nursery with pink and purple floral everywhere.

"He had this done when he found out. He's convinced it's a girl." She sat on the couch in the far corner and patted the seat beside her. "Every day, he comes in here and sits in that rocking chair, reading baby books." She pointed to the rocking chair sitting beside the crib and let out a tiny laugh. "I try to tell him that you never learn how to be a parent until years later, but he still comes here every day with a new book in hand."

She wiped a tear that had fallen from her eye. "Would you believe me if I told you that Vincent used to be a good man?"

I looked up at her and shook my head. Vincent was and always would be the devil in my eyes.

"It's hard to believe, but it's true. I never knew about Stephanie, not until long after Emmett, and when I told him I was pregnant, he was so happy. He went to all my doctor's appointments and treated me like a queen. He was overjoyed when we found out it was a boy, and for the first couple of months of Emmett's life, Vincent was a good father.

"It wasn't until Emmett turned one that something inside of Vincent flipped. I will never excuse what Vincent has done because he has done some horrible things, but he had a rough life.

I think that, in the end, he let all of his resentments overpower him, and he became so jaded."

She got up and walked to the crib, fixing the blanket that was draped over the railing. "I always knew that one day it would come to that point for him. I would like to say that the shift happened overnight, but I knew it was coming. Every day he would get a little worse until one day, he became almost unrecognizable.

"I guess what I'm trying to say, Rose, is that you have been through hell and back, but letting go of internal anger is not for anyone but yourself. You and Emmett are not like Vincent. Vincent gave up on his happiness. I don't want that for the two of you."

I got what she was saying, I did, but I just wasn't ready.

I picked up one of the teddy bears beside me and let out a breath, not looking up. "Before all of this, I was ready to start over with him. I was on the path to forgive him for what he had done to me. He still wasn't my Emmett, but I figured he would eventually let the wall down, and the old him would come back. I was ready to try to find our happiness again, but now I'm just so mad. Mad at my father for taking a position he doesn't even want. Mad at my mom for being a shell for two years, mad at Sammy for giving his life for mine, mad at Emmett for letting me down when he was the only thing holding me up, but most of all? I'm mad at myself because I know that no matter what, I'll always forgive him, and that's not fair. I just keep getting knocked down over and over, and I just want it to stop. One day I might not be able to get back up, and for the sake of my babies, I need to be strong. I love your son so much, but I don't know if that's enough."

When I was met with silence, I looked up and saw that it was no longer Emilia standing in the room but Emmett.

He walked to where I was sitting on the couch and dropped

to his knees in front of me. "There are no words to describe how sorry I am, Rose, and as much as I want to, I can't rewrite the past."

Yeah. Tell me about it.

He looked around the room and sighed. "I don't know what exactly has me thinking the baby will be a girl. I guess a part of me thinks this is my redemption. A second chance to be a better man to the important women in my life. I let you and my mom down, but I'll die before I let my daughter down."

I didn't respond, and even if I'd wanted to, I didn't think I could. As Emmett gave me little pieces of his thoughts and feelings, I didn't speak. Not because I thought it was bullshit but for fear that he would shut down again, and his wall would return.

He gave me one last glance before getting up. "I'm glad you're coming back. I'll give you some space. I can stay at my old house a little while longer. I know you need time, so I'll give it to you." He turned to leave, and I couldn't help but feel disappointed.

Is that what I really wanted? To be left alone? I knew he had been talking to me more, but it was only because I was pregnant.

I wanted him to fight for me. To tell me he didn't want space, that he wanted me back.

I didn't know what I expected exactly, but it wasn't this.

CHAPTER
Thirty-One

Rose

THE DOORBELL RANG, AND I WAS UTTERLY CONFUSED. For one, I didn't know we even had a doorbell, and two, who was even allowed through the gates but not able to get into the house?

I was in the middle of making lunch for everyone when Lorenzo flew into the room, scaring the shit out of me, and I dropped the slice of ham I had in my hand.

"Who the fuck is that?" he asked, pulling his gun out.

I shrugged and bent down to get the ham that had fallen. "No idea."

He pulled out his phone and called the guys at the gate, but nobody answered. "I'm going to go look. Don't move."

Usually, I wouldn't just obey him so easily, but these sandwiches weren't going to make themselves, so I stayed put. I heard Lorenzo answer the door, but then it was quiet. I didn't hear any guns go off, so I peeked around the corner to see who it was and relaxed when I saw it was Claire.

I ran over and squeezed past Lorenzo, who was currently frozen, looking at her belly. It had only been two weeks since I'd seen Claire, but damn, her belly had grown a lot in that time.

"What happened?" I asked, pulling her into the house and bringing her into the kitchen.

She took a seat at the counter and frowned. "I told my parents, and they kicked me out."

"Seriously? For being pregnant? That's a little extreme." I finished putting the rest of the sandwich together and slid it over for whenever Lorenzo became unfrozen. I grabbed the chicken salad sandwich I'd made for myself and placed it in front of her.

She shrugged in response, taking a bite. "I guess it's not a good look."

Ever since I'd known Claire, her mother had been obsessed with their image. She was a "don't eat that, don't touch that, and don't speak unless spoken to" type. Everything had to be perfect, and anything less was unacceptable.

"Fuck that. Good thing this house has, like, thirty rooms." I winked at her.

She shook her head and put the sandwich down. "Oh, no, I can't intrude like that. That's not why I came here. I just didn't want to be alone right now."

"So, what? You're going to move into an apartment and be alone every day with a baby? Yeah, I don't think so. If it makes you feel any better, I can talk to Emmett, and he can confirm that it's all right."

She thought it over for a bit and finally nodded. "Okay, if it's okay with you and Emmett, then I would love to move in."

I went around the counter and pulled her in for a hug. "Let's go to his office, and we can talk to him right now."

The ride to Montgomery Mining was spent in silence. Not one word was spoken, and the radio off. The silence felt heavy, almost deadly. During the ride, I searched for any type of sound, but I got nothing.

Once we parked, I opened my door to get out of the car. Typically, I waited for Lorenzo to get out and come around, but ever since he'd laid eyes on Claire, I think his brain was trying to come up with answers.

I turned around after getting out and opened Claire's door, I was reaching out my hand to help Claire when the sound of a gun cocking back caused my movements to halt.

Lorenzo heard it, too, because he flew out of the driver's seat but stopped when he looked around.

I straightened when I felt cool metal press into the back of my head, and that was when I noticed we were surrounded by too many men to count, each one of them with a gun at their side, ready to go.

Lorenzo lifted his hand just as three men stepped forward, silently daring him to shoot.

I closed the car door, and Lorenzo put his hand down, blocking the other side, both of us hoping Claire would take the hint and stay put.

I turned around to face whoever was holding a gun to my head, but when we made eye contact, I had no idea who the guy was. I raised an eyebrow at him in question, and he just continued to stare me down.

"Something I can help you with?" I moved to cross my arms, but I thought better of it, not wanting to draw attention to my belly.

A flash of surprise then understanding marked the man's features. "Rose Rossi." He smirked at me.

I contemplated lying, saying that he'd gotten the wrong girl, but you wouldn't bring this much backup without doing your research. "Is that a question or a statement?" I leaned back on the car door and propped my foot up.

"Before, it would've been a question, but now? Statement."

"And you are?" I smirked back.

His smirk transformed into a grin. "Carmine Rossi."

Ahh, okay, now it made sense.

Carmine Rossi, head of the Rossi crime family of New York.

Now that he said it, I could see a slight resemblance to Vincent in some of Carmine's facial features. Vincent must've gotten his height from his mother's side, though, because Carmine was at least six feet tall, could be a little less, and his head was bald and shiny as hell, so with the sun reflecting off it, it was kind of hard to tell.

I knew he would come after me, but it had been silent for so long that I'd almost forgotten about it.

"Imagine my surprise"—he lowered the gun and looked me up and down—"when I find out that my cousin was not only killed by a woman but by his daughter-in-law."

"Yeah, well, I don't feel sorry. A life for a life," I bit out.

"And whose life would that be?" he questioned.

"My brother," I snapped back, "but I'm sure you already knew that."

I was glad my back was to Lorenzo, and I couldn't see his face because I knew he was probably not too happy with me right now for the way I was talking to Carmine, but I really didn't care that we were severely outnumbered. If we were in his territory, it would be different, but he was in my territory, and he would do well to remember that.

"Carmine, I don't appreciate you pointing a gun at my wife," Emmett said in a calm, even tone, pushing through the row of men.

"And I don't appreciate my men being killed," Carmine responded, causing me to roll my eyes. "Plus," he continued, "your wife has an attitude."

"Well, she is my daughter," I heard my father's voice come from somewhere else behind me.

"You're early," my father said once he reached us.

"You know I just love the element of surprise," Carmine said, still not taking his eyes off me.

So, he wasn't really here for me. He was here for a meeting. Not going to lie, but I was kind of annoyed that my father and Emmett didn't tell me they were meeting with him. I got that they were trying to protect me, but I would have still liked to have been kept in the loop.

"My office is this way," Emmett growled before walking into the building.

"She comes too." Carmine winked at me before following Emmett.

Carmine brought only two men in with him and left the rest, probably to make sure this wasn't a setup. Lorenzo and Claire followed inside, but Emmett made sure they stayed in the waiting room next to the front desk.

Emmett took a seat behind his desk, my dad stood on his left, and I was on his right.

"Were you aware that my mother is alive?" Emmett started.

A flash of surprise showed on Carmine's face, but he quickly disguised it. "Yes, I was." If it weren't for his slip up of surprise, you would never have known he was lying.

"Then do you know why he faked her death?" Emmett questioned.

"Enlighten me," Carmine responded, taking a seat across from Emmett.

Emmett reached into his desk and pulled out a folder. "My mother found a book that my father kept hidden. Inside, it stated all the business Vincent had been conducting behind your back in your name, but there's more."

After sliding the folder across the desk to Carmine, Emmett pulled out another folder. "Vincent was your middleman, correct? He was in charge of moving the cash from one place to the other?" Carmine stopped looking through the papers, and his head jerked up. Gone was the cocky expression he'd worn earlier. He nodded, and Emmett continued, "Well, this is his record of all the money he pinched and stole from you."

Emmett slid the other folder across the table, and Carmine took a few minutes, looking over every piece of paper.

When he was finished, he looked back up, and I saw the rage in his eyes.

"My mother threatened to send these to you, but my father wouldn't allow it, knowing what you would do to him. So instead, he kept her locked in his basement for years."

Carmine was quiet for a while, probably thinking over his options.

"The way I see it," my father finally spoke, "you can tell your men that Vincent was a thief and had to pay the price."

Carmine gave my father a tight nod and closed the folder.

Giving me one last once-over, he smiled and winked before getting up to leave, my father following behind him.

"That went better than expected." I let out a breath just as the door flung open.

Emmett and I jumped at the sound, and I was wondering if Carmine had changed his mind, but it was Claire who rushed in with Lorenzo right behind her.

"What the hell was that?" Claire and Lorenzo said at the same time, looking between Emmett and me.

"A deal." I shrugged at her before turning to Emmett. "Claire got kicked out. Is it okay if she stays with us at the mansion?"

"Yeah, of course, you didn't have to ask." He smiled at her.

Claire came around his desk to hug him, and he jerked his gaze to Lorenzo when he saw the big pregnant belly she was sporting.

He turned to me with a question in his eyes, and I gave my head a slight shake.

"Well, we better get going." I moved to the door, pulling Claire with me. "I still haven't had lunch."

CHAPTER
Thirty-Two

Emmett

I WALKED INTO THE MANSION AND LOOKED AROUND, TRYING to find Rose, but instead, I found Claire on the couch watching *Coco* and crying.

"Hey, where's Rose?" I asked hesitantly.

Her gaze didn't stray from the TV as she pointed to the set of French doors and sniffled. "Stars."

"Okay, thanks," I replied.

I opened the door and found her outside. She was lying in the grass with a big smile on her face, one hand rubbing her belly while the other was above her head, her hair fanning around her.

It had been two days since the meeting with Carmine, and every time I'd come here, she had either been out with Claire or already in bed.

I stood there for a little bit, just taking in how fucking beautiful she was. I still hated what I had to do to Sammy, but I'd concluded that even though Sammy had been my best friend, if I could go back, I would choose her every time. Seeing Carmine pointing a gun at her head snapped me out of my pity party, and now that I had finally woken the fuck up, nothing was going to stop me from getting my girl back.

I'd given her time and space, but now? I was all in, and I wasn't stopping until I got what I came for.

I walked over and lay down beside her. "Every time I missed you, I would come outside, to this spot actually, and I'd look up at the moon and the stars, just remembering the countless hours we spent together just looking at them."

She ignored my statement and pointed up. "You see that bright star that's right next to the moon?"

I nodded, then remembered it was dark, so she couldn't see me. "Yeah."

"Sammy bought me that star." I couldn't see her, but I could hear the smile in her voice. "He bought it for our sixteenth birthday." She laughed. "He told me I was the moon, and he was the star. He said that no matter what, he would always be right on my ass."

She kept laughing, and I joined her because it was something Sammy would have said.

"I searched for so long for it after he died, but I haven't been able to see it until now. The last time I saw him was the last time I saw the star. It sounds dumb, but I feel like this is a sign that he's with me."

"He's always with you, Rose," I replied. "Just like the stars, just because you can't see them doesn't mean they aren't there."

She was quiet for a while, and it was five long minutes before she spoke again. "I have an ultrasound tomorrow to find out the gender. Do you think you'd wanna come?" she asked, finally turning her head to look at me.

"I would love to." I hovered my hand over her belly, silently asking her permission to touch.

She put her hand over mine and pushed it the rest of the way until I felt the hard, round belly.

We both lay there for a while, just staring at the stars. My hand on our baby, and her hand on mine, neither of us wanting to move.

CHAPTER
Thirty-Three

Emmett

WE FOUND OUT AT THE DOCTOR'S THAT WE WERE having a boy and girl.

Twins.

Fucking twins.

Rose had been so excited ever since the doctor told us, but I was freaking out. I loved seeing them on the screen, don't get me wrong, but I had no idea how to be a father, which hit me hard at the appointment.

Once I realized there were two babies in there, I was hoping for two girls. I had no idea how I was supposed to raise a kid to begin with, especially not a boy.

Girls almost always looked up to their mothers, so I wasn't worried because there wasn't a single doubt in my mind that Rose would be a perfect mother, but a boy? How was I supposed to have someone look up to me?

My father was never anything to go by, and even though I

knew I wouldn't be like him, a part of me was scared I was going to fuck it up in some way.

My thoughts were disrupted when I walked into the kitchen to get a drink and saw Lorenzo and Claire in what looked like a heated discussion.

I'd almost forgotten that Claire had moved in a few days after Rosie came back.

She quickly wiped the tears from her eyes when she saw me, and Lorenzo let out an angry growl before he stomped out of the room.

"You okay?" I took a hesitant step closer to her, trying to get to the fridge.

She let out an aggressive scoff. "I will be, eventually."

I grabbed two bottles of water from the fridge and handed one to her.

"You know, I think a part of him is mad that it's not his baby. Not because he wanted a baby to begin with but because he thought he could go out and fuck all these girls, and I would just sit around, waiting for him to be ready for me."

She moved to open her water bottle, but it slipped from her fingers. I was just about to grab it when I noticed she was swaying.

I reached out to touch her shoulder and steady her, but she completely lost her footing, and I tossed the water bottle so I could catch her just as she started to fall. Her eyes were closed, and I called her name, but she wouldn't wake up.

"Lorenzo," I yelled out, but he must've left because he didn't answer.

I pushed one of the panic buttons hidden in the wall, and two security guys came rushing in.

"I need one of you to call an ambulance and tell them to go through the garage. I need the other to find Rose, and I'll meet you down there."

I scooped up her legs, trying not to jostle her too much, and I raced to the elevator.

Just as the elevator doors opened, Rose hurried toward me. "What the hell happened? Is she okay?"

"I don't know. She just passed out." The elevator opened up to the garage, and we stepped out. After what felt like forever, the ambulance pulled up. I quickly handed Claire over, and they put her on the stretcher.

I turned to one of my guards. "Go with her, and I'll meet you at the hospital." The guard nodded and followed Claire into the ambulance.

"I'll meet you in the car," I said to Rose. "I'm going to grab my phone and call Tommy."

"Okay. I'll try to call her parents." She had a frantic look in her eyes, but before I could make sure she was okay, she was racing into the car.

CHAPTER
Thirty-Four

Rose

THE URGE I HAD RIGHT NOW TO WRAP MY HANDS around someone's throat until they stopped breathing was so strong that anytime someone got close to me, my hands twitched.

Lorenzo was currently at some bar, drinking away his sorrows, Tommy wasn't answering, and Claire's parents refused to come because, according to them, they "no longer have a daughter."

Meanwhile, Claire's water just broke, and the only person by her side was me.

I stopped looking at her unless I had to because every time I did, a new wave of rage hit me. She looked so sad, and I hated that there was nothing I could do about it.

For the first hour that we were here, whenever the door opened, I saw the hope in her eyes that it was her parents or Tommy, but now she didn't even bother to look up.

I didn't have the heart to tell her that her parents had said they wouldn't come, and I was still hoping that Tommy would show up, but I wasn't holding my breath. He was supposed to be at school, but he has been so off lately that he could be in Mexico for all we knew.

The nurse came in to check how dilated she was and told her she was about ten centimeters and would probably be pushing soon.

The doctor came in shortly after, rechecked Claire, and gave her a bright smile. "Looks like you're ready to push. I'm going to suit up, and then we can get started."

She gave him a sad smile and nodded.

Just as the doctor finished suiting up and put his gloves on, the door flew open, and in ran Tommy with a busted lip and what looked like a bruise starting to form on his cheek.

He looked over at Claire and me and gave us his famous smirk. "You didn't think you were going to do this without me, did you? I can't miss the arrival of my nephew."

I looked over at Claire, and I saw her eyes brighten as she said, "It could be a girl. We don't even know yet."

Tommy walked up to her and placed a kiss on her head. "Either way, I wouldn't miss it for the world."

Her smile was so bright that I decided to spare Tommy from the wrath I was ready to unleash on him.

"Ready?" the doctor asked Claire.

She grabbed Tommy's and my hands and took a deep breath. "Ready."

"Okay, now push."

An hour later, Claire's baby girl made her debut, and there wasn't a dry eye in the room. Tommy included.

Even though the baby came a few weeks earlier than her due date, the doctor said the baby looked to be in good health. They had to run some tests, but they allowed Claire to hold her for a little bit before they had to take her.

"You know, I never thought of any names," Claire said, not taking her gaze off her daughter.

Now, say what you wanted about me, but my instincts were usually very much correct, and I think I knew exactly what I needed to do right now.

"How about Delilah?" I suggested, looking down at the baby.

From the corner of my eye, I saw Claire look up at me for half a second before looking back down. "Huh, Delilah, I like it. It's kind of perfect." She grabbed my hand and gave it a small squeeze. "Delilah Rose."

Twenty minutes later, the doctor came in and told Claire they had to take the baby for a little bit.

She sobbed when Delilah was taken to another room, and she couldn't go with her.

Usually, the baby's father would go with the baby, but Tommy went instead since that wasn't an option.

My phone buzzed, and I ran to it, hoping it was Lorenzo.

Emmett: Hey, how's it going in there?

Oh, shit. I'd forgotten that Emmett was still in the waiting room.

"Hey, I have to go and give Emmett an update. I forgot he was in the waiting room." I started for the door, but Claire stopped me with a hand.

"No," Claire said quickly. "Tell him to come up here. I still need to thank him for catching me."

I nodded at her and sent Emmett a text.

Rose: Why don't you come up here? Claire wants to see you.

Emmett: Okay. Be right up.

Ten minutes later, Emmett walked in with about five balloons and a huge bouquet of roses.

"I googled what you give someone who just pushed a baby out of their vagina, and this is what I got." We all started laughing hysterically, and he placed the flowers and balloons on one of the tables.

Claire opened her arms, motioning at him for a hug. "Thank you so much, Emmett. It would've been awful if I'd fallen. I am so grateful for you."

He pulled away and gave her a shrug. "It's no biggie, so don't mention it."

Just then, Tommy returned, rolling Delilah in with him and parking her next to her mom.

"Emmett, meet Delilah Rose." Claire lifted Delilah and gently placed her in Emmett's arms.

His eyes softened when he looked at the tiny baby sleeping in his arms. "She's so beautiful, Claire."

He held Delilah for a long time, just smiling at her until she started fussing.

At the first cry, Emmett's eyes grew wide, and he frantically looked from me to Claire, silently asking us what to do.

Claire laughed and put her hands out. "She's probably hungry."

"And that's our cue to leave. Let's go grab some food because Uncle Tommy's hungry too," Tommy said, slapping Emmett's shoulder and rubbing his stomach.

I handed Claire a bottle, and ten minutes later, Delilah was fed, and all three of us decided it was nap time.

CHAPTER
Thirty-Five

Rose

IT HAD BEEN A FULL TWO WEEKS SINCE DELILAH WAS BORN and I'd banished Lorenzo from showing his face. After he groveled nonstop, I was finally giving in and lifting the banishment.

He was MIA for a whole twenty-four hours after his fight with Claire, and when he finally reemerged from the depths of his indiscretions, he had to call Emmett to pick him up because he had no idea where he even was, let alone where he'd left his car.

He must have known he'd fucked up because he didn't even bother to fight me when I told him he needed to stay somewhere else for a few days.

I was making lunch for everyone when I heard the elevator ding, followed by some heavy footsteps, and the next thing I knew, I was being hugged from behind.

I froze at the feel of someone touching me until I realized it was actually Lorenzo.

"I never thought being without everyone for two weeks would feel so lonely." He sighed.

A pang of guilt hit me when I remembered that aside from us, Lorenzo was truly alone. Frowning, I pulled away and turned around.

I knew Lorenzo hated that he was so alone, so after Emmett and I got married, Lorenzo moved out of his apartment and into one of the many rooms here. Since then, I'd noticed he'd been a lot happier.

When he'd lived alone, he used to constantly take girls home for the night, and I always wondered if it was more to do with him not wanting to be alone and less to do with him wanting to sleep around.

At the sight of my huge belly, Lorenzo's eyes went wide.

"Oh, shit, Rosie, you grew."

I narrowed my eyes at him. "Thanks. Because that's something a severely pregnant woman wants to hear."

He laughed and pulled me in for another hug. "You know I'm just teasing."

A throat clearing sounded, and I pulled away to see Emmett standing in the doorway, glaring at us.

"Stop touching my wife, Moretti," Emmett growled.

"Suck it, Rossi." Lorenzo smirked. "You wish you were as close to her as I am. I've been with her every day for seven years. Two weeks away from her felt like a century, and I missed her. Sue me."

Emmett ignored him and turned to me, lifting an empty baby bottle in the air and shaking it. "Claire didn't want to disturb you guys, so she sent me to grab some more milk for Delil—"

"Okay," I yelled, cutting him off from finishing her name. "I'll show you."

His eyebrows pinched together, and I looked over to see a

deep frown on Lorenzo's face. I would have to tell Emmett later not to say Delilah's name in front of Lorenzo. I knew he would find out her name eventually, but it wasn't our place to be the ones to tell him.

I grabbed the milk that Claire had already pumped out of the fridge, and I warmed it up, handing it back to Emmett.

"Please tell Claire I'll be there in a minute."

He grabbed the bottle and left the room, shaking his head.

"You hungry?" I asked Lorenzo, turning back to the sandwiches I was making.

"Yes, please." He took a seat and started fidgeting with his shirt. "How is she?" he asked without looking up.

"Claire or the baby?" I asked.

He shrugged a shoulder and let out a soft sigh. "Both, I guess."

I cut his sandwich in half and placed it in front of him. "Why don't you go find her and ask?"

He looked up at me and shrugged again. "She doesn't wanna see me."

"I love you, Lorenzo. You're like a brother to me, but I wanna punch you in the throat. Don't be a jackass."

He didn't respond and took a bite of his sandwich, ending the conversation.

I wished they would just open their eyes and see what was in front of them. Was this how people felt when they looked at Emmet and me? Because, if so, I felt terrible. This was frustrating.

CHAPTER
Thirty-Six

Rose

Now that the threat from the Rossi family in New York was gone, I could finally leave the house without ten security guards and visit Sammy. It was our birthday today, and I was grateful that I could go alone. Well, still with Lorenzo, but at least now he could give me space.

We went to Sammy's favorite bakery and got in line to order the cupcakes, and just as we were about to order, I felt a tap on my shoulder.

I turned around to see Victoria Diego standing there. As if this day wasn't already hard enough.

"Do you have a minute?" she asked.

I contemplated saying no and telling her to go fuck herself, but something in her eyes had me nodding.

Lorenzo nodded, already knowing the order, and I moved to the side with her, sitting at one of the nearby tables.

"I'm sorry," she blurted out, "for everything."

I didn't reply, just continued to stare.

"I never told anyone, but when I was sixteen, I was attacked. I'm not going to go into detail because I'm not ready for that." She took a deep breath, and I could tell this was really hard for her to say, so I put my hand out and placed it on her arm.

"You don't have to tell me this," I said to her.

"No, I do. I know that what happened to me is not an excuse for what I've said and done, but I'd like to explain myself." She looked up at me before continuing, "I was horrible to you in high school, and at first, it was just me being a jealous bitch, but after the attack, well, I was still a jealous bitch, but I think I was also just looking for someone take my anger out on, and it was you."

She took another deep breath and closed her eyes. "After high school, I had no one to pick on, so I would just start drinking a lot. One night, I was at a club, and I saw Emmett. I practically threw myself at him, but he rejected me. I don't remember what happened after that, but I guess he found me twenty minutes later, slumped in a corner. He got me a room at a nearby hotel and left me there to sleep and sober up. The next morning, he came back and asked me what was going on, and I finally exploded. I told him everything, and by the end, he hugged me and tried to persuade me to talk to my parents about it, but I refused. After that, he checked on me sometimes and made sure I was okay. That night at your engagement party, I drank again, and I went back to being the jealous bitch from high school. After you hit me, which I one hundred percent deserved, Emmett helped me up and told me it was time to talk to someone. I took his advice and finally told my parents. I see a therapist now, and I'm working through things."

She finally opened her eyes and looked at me.

"You didn't deserve the awful things I said about your brother, and I am so sorry."

I went around the table and pulled her in for a hug.

"It's okay," I whispered, and she put her arms around me too. I felt her jolt in surprise, probably at the large pregnant belly I had under this sweater, but she just continued to hug me.

I was surprised at how easily I forgave her. Maybe it was because today marked four years since I lost my brother, or maybe it was because my views had changed, but either way, life was too short for me to hold grudges. I couldn't keep living my life with so much resentment. It was time to move forward.

My visit with Sammy was shorter than usual. My belly was so big, it was hard for me to sit on the ground for too long, and after half an hour, I couldn't take it anymore.

Walking into the living room, I saw Claire and Delilah playing on the floor with cartoons on in the background.

It was the biggest room in the house, and Delilah loved the open space and being surrounded by toys, but Claire only came out here when Lorenzo wasn't home.

I kept telling her that she couldn't avoid him forever, considering they lived in the same house, but she just kept brushing me off.

"Hey." Claire smiled when she looked up and saw me. "I made you an ice cream cookie sandwich. It's in the freezer, so you should grab it before someone eats it."

Every year on my birthday, Claire made me a homemade ice cream cookie sandwich. She knew not to go all out because my birthday was a hard day for me, but she always did this to show her love, and I was grateful.

"Thank you." I smiled at her. "I'm gonna go lay down. I'm not feeling it today, but call me if you need anything."

She gave me a sad smile. "Okay. Tommy should be here in a little bit. He's taking us to dinner if you want to join us."

"Thank you, but I'll be okay."

She nodded at me, and I planted a kiss on hers and Delilah's heads.

A few hours later, I was still up, looking outside my window at the stars, when I saw a shadow stop outside my door.

Every night like clockwork, Emmett came home from the office and sat outside my door for hours. Normally, I ignored it, but tonight, I didn't want to be alone.

Walking up to the door and opening it, I found him sitting against the wall across from my door, and he jumped up when he saw me.

I put my hand out for him to take it. "Come look at the stars with me."

He gently placed his hand in mine and smiled, letting me lead him into the room. He pushed my bed against the wall next to the window and motioned for me to lay down.

With me on the inside and Emmett on the outside, he gently placed his hand on my belly, and we both looked out the window.

I was starting to drift off to sleep when I felt Emmett kiss the hair behind my ear, and I heard him whisper, "Happy birthday, Rosie."

That night, I fell asleep with a smile.

CHAPTER
Thirty-Seven

Rose

I WOKE UP IN THE MORNING IN A PUDDLE OF WATER AND MY pants soaked. It took a full three minutes of mental debate before I finally concluded my water had broken.

And cue the freak-out.

I jumped out of bed when the realization hit, causing Emmett to shoot up, and then we were both freaking out.

And that, my friends, was what brought me to this exact moment.

"My water broke. We have to go. Like right now," I rushed out.

"Shit." He jumped out of bed, and I got a full view of his hot as hell naked body.

Well. That certainly distracted me from my frantic episode real quick. It was too dark when he climbed into bed last night, so I didn't get to see him until now.

An excruciating contraction hit me, and I snapped out of my stupor, hunching over in pain.

He rushed to my side and wrapped his arms around me, and I felt his naked body pressed into me.

"Yeah, we have to go, big boy." I tried to laugh, but the pain still wasn't subsiding, so it came out as an ugly gurgle instead.

He threw some pants and a shirt on and quickly ushered me to the elevator.

"Wait." I stopped moving. "We need to get Lorenzo." When he lifted a brow and opened his mouth, probably to argue, I cut him off. "He has been with me for this whole pregnancy. He deserves to be there."

I instantly regretted the words when Emmett flinched and looked down.

"I'm sorry," I said, placing my finger under his chin and lifting his head up. "That was a low blow. I know you've been trying, and I didn't mean it like that, so I'm sorry."

He nodded and wrapped his hand around the finger that was still under his chin, then pulled me closer to him. He bent down and placed a kiss on my cheek. "It's okay. I'll get Lorenzo. I'll be right back."

He placed another kiss on my cheek and ran off toward Lorenzo's room. Less than a minute later, Emmett was walking in long strides back to me, and Lorenzo was hopping down the hall, trying to put his shoes on and walk at the same time.

I started to laugh, but then another contraction slammed into me. Emmett rushed over, closing the distance between us, and I grabbed both his arms and hunched over.

When the contraction was over, Emmett tossed his keys to Lorenzo and wrapped an arm around me. "You drive. We have to go."

Lorenzo nodded, and we made our way to the elevators, but I stopped again.

"Wait," I called to them. "We can't just leave without telling Claire."

Emmett nodded and ran back down the hall, coming back again seconds later. "Okay, anything else?" he asked.

I shook my head, and then he wrapped his arm around me again. "Okay, let's go."

We rushed to the car and got to the hospital in record time. The nurse at the front desk took one look at us before escorting us right up to the maternity ward and into a room.

Here goes nothing.

Two hours and an emergency C-section later, Samuel and Madison Rossi were born.

They were born October twenty-six, the day after Sammy's and my birthday.

Madison had a lot of Emmett's features. I'd seen a few pictures of him as a baby, and Madison was all him. The only thing of mine she had was her black hair.

Samuel, though? Well, I guess I chose the correct name because he looked almost identical to Sammy and nothing like Emmett and me.

After the nurses cleaned him up, I held my son and cried happy tears for hours at being able to see that face again.

Emmett, on the other hand? He wouldn't even look at his son for more than ten seconds at a time, let alone hold him.

I could see the battle in his eyes. I knew he wanted to, but he wouldn't allow himself to, and that broke my heart. He just continued to sit in the corner and only grabbed Madison when

I needed help. No matter how many times I told him that it was okay, he looked at me and just frowned.

It wasn't until the last day in the hospital that he finally gave in and held his son.

My eyes flew open when I went to put my hands on my babies, and I only felt one. Quickly scanning the room, I found Emmett carrying Samuel before taking a seat on the couch.

"Shh," he whispered, "we have to let your mom sleep, okay? Just for a few more hours. She's really tired." Taking a deep breath, he continued, "You know, you look just like your Uncle Sammy. I'd be jealous if I didn't miss him so much."

Madison started to fuss, and he looked up, catching me watching him.

"Sorry," I said while lifting Madison and cradling her in my arms. "I just didn't expect to see you holding him. I wanted to savor the view."

"It's all right." He shrugged. "I hate myself for waiting so long, but I never expected him to look just like Sammy." Emmett brushed his hand gently over Samuel's head, trying to flatten some of the hair that was sticking up. "After Sammy died, I had nightmares every night where I was back at that warehouse with a gun in my hand and Sammy tied up in front of me. The last thing I'd see before I woke up was his face when the bullet pierced his skin. Eventually, I just forced myself to stay awake most nights, so I didn't have the nightmare."

Emmett moved to hold Samuel's hand, and Samuel wrapped his hand around Emmett's finger, causing him to smile.

"I'd always planned on telling you. I knew you would hate me for a little while, but I told myself that you would forgive me eventually and that it would be okay because you would understand. But the night before the funeral, when we had sex for the first time? Well, that was the first night I had the nightmare, and damn if that didn't change my view. I woke to your naked body wrapped around me, and I hated myself. I hated myself for taking something I sure as hell didn't deserve. I stared at you for what must've been hours until you woke up, trying to figure out a way to resolve this, to fix things, but I just kept coming to the same conclusion. I didn't deserve you. How is it fair that I get to move on with my life with you by my side when he couldn't? I took that opportunity away from him. So, I did what I felt I deserved. For two years, I watched from afar and drank myself half to death on many occasions because I didn't deserve the feeling of happiness and pure bliss that came with you, and I sure as hell didn't deserve your forgiveness."

"But that wasn't your decision to make," I finally spoke up. "You may not feel like it, but it wasn't your fault. You're punishing yourself for something that you had no control over. It comes down to the fact that you had two choices, and they both ended horribly. It was Sammy or me. And if you had told me back then? I would've understood. I would've forgiven you, but you never gave me the chance."

Emmett got up and gently placed Samuel in the bassinet, then took Madison from me and laid her beside Samuel before taking both my hands in his.

"You're right, and I regret not telling you, trust me. There's nothing I can do about the past, but I can do something about our future, I promise." He planted a kiss on my forehead and let go of my hands. "I'll be right back, okay?"

I nodded, and he kissed the babies before he left.

Emmett was gone for most of the morning, only to come back an hour before it was time to leave.

"You got everything?" he asked, strapping Samuel into his car seat.

I looked around one last time, and I was about to ask him how we would carry everything, including the babies, when Lorenzo walked in with a huge grin on his face.

He kissed me on my head, then walked up to Madison and picked her up. "How are you feeling?" He turned to me and asked before kissing Madison and gently placing her in her car seat.

Emmett growled at Lorenzo and shooed him away. "Leave my wife and daughter alone. Help with the bags and flowers."

Lorenzo rolled his eyes. "You sound like a broken record, Rossi."

"Well then, maybe you should stop touching my wife, Moretti," Emmett scoffed.

The nurse came in, interrupting their banter, and asked, "Everything all set?"

"Yes." I smiled at her. "Ready to go."

She led us out of the room and down the elevator to a waiting car at the entrance.

We all hopped in. Lorenzo was driving, Emmett was in the front, and I was in the back between the babies.

The ride home was uneventful. Emmett and Lorenzo were in the front arguing per usual, and the babies were asleep the whole ride.

We pulled into the garage, and Emmett hopped out first, grabbing Madison, then went around to grab Samuel while Lorenzo took all the bags and ran inside.

I walked in the house first, turning to Emmett when I'd

opened the door, and didn't hear kids running around. "Isn't Stephanie here? I wanted her to see the twins."

Stephanie didn't have a chance to visit us at the hospital. She had been taking some GED classes online, and between classes and the kids, she didn't have time for anything these days.

He shrugged his shoulders, and I kept moving forward.

Turning the corner to go into the living room, I jumped back when I heard a loud whispered, "Welcome home."

I looked to see my mom and dad, Claire, Delilah, Tommy, Lorenzo, Emilia, Stephanie, and all of Emmett's siblings looking back at me with bright smiles, and my eyes instantly filled with tears.

I turned back to Emmett, and he placed the car seats down gently on the floor and gave me a shrug. "I knew today would be hard for you, and the only way that I know I can make you smile is by bringing together the people you love most." He laced his fingers with mine, and I saw my mom and Emilia had already pulled Madison and Samuel out of their car seats.

I said hi to everyone and gave them quick hugs. I looked over at my mom and saw her on one of the couches, holding Samuel with the biggest smile on her face.

"I haven't seen your mother smile like that in years," my father said, coming up behind me.

"He looks like Sammy," I replied with a smile of my own.

"They're beautiful, Rosie," my father said, not taking his eyes off my mom.

I looked up at him and wrapped my arms around him for the first time since Sammy had died. "I'm sorry for blaming you all these years. You did the best you could, and I understand that now. You were right about bringing Emmett back into my life. It had to get hard before it got easier, and I'm grateful for your push."

My father gave me a gentle squeeze before pulling away. "Thank you." He smiled back at me, and I swear I saw the tiniest bit of moisture building in his eyes before he turned away.

"Go see her," I told him, pointing my head at my mom.

He gave my arm one last squeeze before nodding and walking away.

I watched as he hesitantly approached her, and she looked up at him, her smile never wavering. I looked over to see Claire on the other couch, sitting with Tommy while he played with Delilah, and I was about to go to them when Emmett stepped in front of me.

"Do you have a minute?" he asked, rubbing his hands on his pants.

I double-checked to make sure the twins were in good hands before I nodded and allowed him to lead me down the hall, and he stopped at his bedroom.

"I hope you don't mind, but I wanted Madison to have her own room, so I made one for Samuel."

He opened the door, and my jaw dropped when I looked around.

The whole room décor was themed with the moon and stars, even down to a beautiful night sky painted on the ceiling.

"I love it," I whispered to him.

He grabbed my hand, walked me to the room end of the hall, and opened the door.

I looked around and saw a huge master bedroom with what had to be a custom-size bed in the middle.

"I had the room reconstructed for us to have private entrances into the babies' rooms, but I also added this." He walked into the walk-in closet and opened up another door that led to the library. He placed his hands over my eyes and walked me a few feet forward before turning my body and whispering in my ear, "Are you ready?"

I nodded, and he slowly pulled his hands away. I opened my eyes, tears instantly forming when I saw a huge portrait of Sammy and me on our seventeenth birthday.

This was my favorite picture of us. Everyone said that a picture was worth a thousand words, but this one was worth two thousand.

We had an arm around each other, and my head was tilted up while he was hunched over, both of us in a fit of laughter. We were trying to take a serious picture, but Sammy kept cracking joke after joke, and after five minutes, Claire just took one and called it a day.

"I love it. Thank you so much." I turned to Emmett, ready to throw my arms around him, when he grabbed my hand, pulled the ring off my finger, and sank onto one knee.

He took a deep breath before looking up at me. "Five years ago, I bought this ring for the love of my life. You see, she made a promise to me that when she turned eighteen, we would run off and get married, but everything got fucked up. I hope I'm not too late, but Rose Maria Rossi, would you do me the honor of marrying me? The right way this time?"

I pulled him up, pressing my head to his, and he wiped the tears that were currently streaming down my face. I looked into his eyes, and I saw a color that I never thought I'd see again.

"I missed those blues," I whispered at him, and he smirked. I pulled away and held my hand out to him. "Of course, I will. I thought you'd never ask."

He slid the ring back on my finger, and I slammed my lips onto his. That was when I heard a loud whistle and clapping.

We pulled apart, and I looked over to see everyone squished in the doorway, watching us.

Emmett threw his arm out and motioned for everyone to come in, and the next thing I knew, Claire, Tommy, and Lorenzo were throwing their arms around Emmett and me, forming a big-ass group hug.

I looked over at our parents holding all the babies and then up at Sammy's portrait, and I couldn't help but smile because, in that moment, everything felt lighter.

CHAPTER
Thirty-Eight

Emmett

ROSE'S MOM AND DAD LEFT, AND EVERYONE ELSE WENT to their wings in the mansion, leaving just Rosie and me with the twins.

"Do you think we could go somewhere really quick?" I asked her.

She nodded her head, and we put Samuel and Madison into their car seats, quickly telling Claire and Lorenzo that we would be right back.

Twenty minutes later, I pulled into the entrance of the cemetery.

"What are we doing here?" Rose asked.

"There's someone I need to talk to. I think it's been long overdue." I stopped right next to Sammy's spot and turned to Rose. "Wait here for a second."

I got out of the car and finally faced his gravestone.

"Hey, Sammy." I took a deep breath. "I'm sorry for being too much of a pussy to come to see you. And I'm sorry for breaking our promise and hurting Rose after you died." I took a seat and stared at the picture of him that was on the headstone. "I know it's a late apology, but you did always say that I was the slowest fucker you'd ever met." I chuckled.

"I have to make this quick because it's getting late, but I just want to say thank you. Thank you for being my best fucking friend—actually, fuck that. Thank you for being my brother." I let out a sigh and moved to stand. "I have some people I want you to meet."

I ran to the car and grabbed Madison. "Can you get Samuel out and follow me?" I asked Rose.

I walked back to the stone and smiled at my daughter. "This is your niece, Madison Claire Rossi. She looks just like me, so you already know she's going to be a stunner. I'm definitely gonna be in trouble with her when she's older, but I'll worry about that when I have to."

Rose walked toward me with Samuel, and I smiled at them when she reached me.

"And this, well, this is your nephew, Samuel John Rossi. He looks just like you. I couldn't even face him when he was born. I guess a part of me never let go of what happened, but I'm getting better. I was a shell for a long time, but not anymore. I promise I'll do right by your sister and our kids. There's no other option."

Samuel started to fuss, and Rose bounced him a little bit to soothe him.

"I have to go, but I'll be back. We have some catching up to do."

After walking back to the car, we buckled them back in their seats and hopped back in.

"Are you okay?" Rosie grabbed my hand and gave it a slight squeeze.

I reached over and planted a soft kiss onto her lips.

"I'm perfect."

Epilogue

Rose

TODAY WAS THE TWINS' BIRTHDAY, AND WE WERE throwing a little party to celebrate. I couldn't believe they were already one.

I also couldn't believe that Emmett and I will be married for two years in two weeks. We haven't had our redo, but I wasn't entirely sure if I even wanted one.

To think that two years ago, I was at one of my lowest points and about to get married but now look at us.

Peeking out the window, I caught a glimpse of Emmett and the twins in the backyard, chasing the puppy we'd just gotten them for their birthday, and I couldn't help but stop to watch.

The twins had gotten so big. Samuel had started walking two months ago, and Madison had started walking a few weeks ago, so she was still a little rusty, but Emmett was always right there, waiting to catch her if she fell. Madison was definitely a daddy's girl.

Samuel, however, well, that boy was a tank. Nobody believed

me when I told them he was only one because he towered over his sister and was built like a three-year-old. He was quiet for the most part, always looking around and observing his surroundings.

Madison was the talker, though. I could tell her middle name was perfect because she definitely had her Auntie Claire's negotiation skills, and even though we couldn't understand her, I knew she was arguing.

Looking at the three of them together, I could finally say I'd found my purpose.

Although there was still a piece of me missing, I would always keep Sammy's memory alive, and I couldn't wait to tell my kids all the stories of their parents and uncle growing up.

It still hurt, and I still missed Sammy so fucking much, but I'd learned to accept how my life had turned out.

Happily-ever-after doesn't come easy. You need to keep fighting, even when you don't want to anymore. In the end, you'll find that all the bruises were worth it.

The End

Author's note

First, I want to say thank you so much for reading! This book took a lot out of me, and I really hope you enjoyed it.

I started writing this book in a notebook late one night when I couldn't sleep, and I'd probably made it through one chapter before my hand started getting tired, so I grabbed my computer and started typing.

I had no idea what the book was going to be about, but the more I wrote, the more the story became clear. I wrote on and off, and after about a year and a half of deleting and rewriting so many things, I finally feel it is finished.

As much as this story will always be my baby, I'm glad it's over—now onto our boy Tommy.

Follow me on Instagram for updates!
@v.books11

Acknowledgments

Readers: Thank you for giving this book a read! I can't wait to write more, and I hope you like this one enough to give my next one a chance!

My fiancé: Thank you for being a pain in my ass and everything I will ever need. You mean more to me than you'll ever know. I love you forever.

My parents: Thank you for letting me turn one of your rooms into a cool-ass office and for birthing me, I guess. You guys are the best.

My sister: Thank you for hyping me up, and you're welcome for having a cool-ass sister who's an author now! And don't worry, I will name a character after you one day. She just has to be a Cancer with a Scorpio moon, and those are complex characters to write, so I have to get a little better at this whole writing thing before I do that.

My girl Sabrina: Thank you for being a loyal-ass bitch and the best book bestie a girl could ever ask for! You are the real MVP. Also, Tommy is yours, I promise.

Madison: Thank you for taking the time to read even though you are busy and thank you for being my girlfriend (sorry Tim) but really, thanks for being the best friend I never knew I needed. And thank you for buttering me up like a lobster. I would say bread, but lobster is more expensive, and so am I.